ONE DEAD GIRL

KRISTEN TRU

ONE DEAD GIRL

Contents

Dedicated to my family and my husband for passionately and, most of the time, blindly supporting everything I've ever done.

Dead

Death is not the end, but it can be a terrible beginning.

I watched my boyfriend, Ash, pile a meatball sandwich in his mouth like it might disappear between his fingers. I thought about how much I loved him in moments like this, with the sauce running down his cheek and chunks of meat missing his mouth. Something about him looked so vulnerable or imperfect that it made me feel closer to him.

The sandwich shop we were at, Bear Station, was a local favorite ran primarily by kids from our high school. It felt like a safe place for all the teens in the area. When I started thinking about leaving for college, I started taking in the shop's small details in the hopes that I would memorize it. I started taking an extra moment to take in the smell you breathed in when you first walked inside. I would look closely at the black and white photos on the wall from the 1950s just to see if there was anything new, anything I'd missed over the years. My favorite part of the sub shop was the large maroon booths that would fit ten if you squeezed really tight, which we always loved to do anyway. When I sat in them, I felt the leather's touch and noted its both smooth and rugged feel across my fingertips.

The first time I ever came to this shop was with Ash, on one of our very first dates. We squeezed together in one of those ten-person booths. Ash chased me for a long time. Once he had me, I couldn't stop chasing him, and I tripped the entire way.

On one of our first dates, he asked me how my day was, and I told him I went to the mountains. He asked me whether he could kiss me, and I told him it was good. He took things slow with me until I could hold a conversation again. He was patient until he switched from being the root of my nerves to being the only person who could ever calm them. I considered kissing him right then as I remembered this, meatball sub mouth and all.

Ash sat in the booth with a couple of his friends. We were all laughing at his friend Alan's most recent attempt at picking up a girl. Alan was born to be a jock; he looked like he was born to play football every Sunday. Instead, he leaned more into music. He played bass in a local band and despised all sports, much to his parents' disappointment.

His love life was also a good laugh, which was not really what anyone wanted their love life to be, but he took what he could get, which were no girls but a couple of chuckles from his buddies.

I watched over them all laughing at Alan, with a sort of peace. The peace wasn't even interrupted when Ash's phone began vibrating on the table ominously. I barely even noticed it at first. It kept shaking, and I began to stare at it, with a feeling in my gut that that phone would take everything from me. Ash looked at it with vulnerable eyes and saw it was a number he didn't recognize and ignored it.

The phone stopped, and I skeptically tried to return to that heavy peace. The phone started shaking the entire table, and this time even paused their conversation.

"Ash, aren't you going to get that?"

Ash grabbed the phone off the table and answered it, annoyed with the interruption. He moved out of the booth and stood just off to the side. He picked it up and said hello, but soon after, the phone slid out of his hands like soap. It smashed into the old red tile floor of the diner—the peace that filled me only a moment before, shattered with his phone on the ground.

His friends tried to ask Ash what happened. But their voices seemed to drown out, and everything suddenly felt like a dream. Alan picked up the broken phone and tried to talk to Ash; in words, I suddenly couldn't understand.

Then Alan put the shattered phone up to his ear and spoke to someone, while our friends continued to try to get Ash to talk. They sat him down in the booth and ordered him water. Ash stared straight ahead and didn't move. He tried to speak once but failed.

Alan turned to us and said, "Sita's dead."

Alan took Ash, who forgot how to move, and with another friend, guided him out to Alan's car. He drove us both to Ash's home in complete silence. I grasped and grasped towards Ash as he moved, but my arms and hands just kept running through him.

They told me I was dead. Still, I was more worried about Ash than I was for myself. You never really know how you're going to react to the news that you're dead until you hear it. My reaction was a haunting need to be there for him. Before Ash and I met, we were both largely on our own. My parents had already passed, and his mother already killed most of her brain cells with alcohol. The thing about two people truly alone finding each other is that they become almost impossible to separate once they are together.

I thought about what this all meant for Ash. I thought about our future together. I thought about us going to college and pursuing our dreams. I thought about us having children and naming them after his grandfather. I thought about our plans next summer to go to Hawaii. But most of all, I thought about whether Ash would be strong enough to live without me.

We pulled up to Ash's duplex, a salmon-colored home in the type of neighborhood where you couldn't walk your dog without some sort of protection. He pulled the keys out of his pocket and got out of the car. "Hey man, slow down, let me help you inside." But Ash turned around and waved him off.

He lived here with his mother when she would stop by, usually drunk. But he paid all the bills and struggled to make ends meet by working full time at the local movie theater. His mother probably wasn't home, as usual, but he couldn't be too careful. The last thing he wanted to do was talk to his drunken mother and somehow work out how to trick her into going to bed, eat some bread, or drink some water.

He went straight up to the bedroom, shut the door, and locked it. First, he just stood there with his back to the door for a moment. I stared at him like he'd stared at me on our very first date, with love and almost desperation. Then he began walking to the bed. He didn't make it. He lost it, lost any and all of the restraint he had created to make it home. He fell on his knees, then to the floor like a Jenga game, all at once and with power. I followed him to the ground and tried to embrace him as hard as I could. I grasped at him but only felt air. I cried tears that never came and screamed words that would never be heard.

Since that day, I have stayed with Ash both day and night. This wasn't by choice, although I would have been with him anyway if I had had a choice. I found absolute comfort in my time with him, but I also knew I shouldn't be here. Something felt wrong. The issue with escaping this undead life was that it is complicated. It was even more complicated if the human you are attached to was drowning in sorrow. Maybe if Ash had gotten his ass out of bed occasionally, I would have learned something new.

Instead, I was stuck. I stared at my sweet boyfriend as he slept and cried and slept and cried. I had no one to talk to, no one to hold, and I couldn't comfort the one person I cared about. All I had was this one dirty and cobwebbed window. It faced out towards the back of a neighbor's house.

I spent so many nights and days in this room, cuddled up in those sheets, now tainted with tears. Laying across Ash's chest as we talked about the world for hours on end. Yet somehow, I never really looked out this window. This view was, at first, a welcome relief. It was a sign that change and life still existed at all. I could look out of it and maybe see a bird fly by or a leaf blew into the yard. I waited for moments like this, moments when I could tell that the Earth was still moving outside of this dreaded room. But now, after what seemed like weeks, I hated it.

I hated things when I was alive. Most notable, Geese, who are good for nothing, little shits that act like they run the world. Another notable hate, Ash's mother, Theresa, a drunk with a special animosity towards me. I hated my aunt, and I hated Ash's manager, who we called a meanager. I could write lists for miles of all the things I hated. Now at the top of that list was the back of Ash's neighbor's house. It was a strange hate, but when you look at something long enough, if you don't love it, you begin to despise it. I despised the small deck they had attached, the brown fence distorted towards the bottom, the off-white shutters that were always closed.

Love has a way of making you feel human. But hate, on the other hand, hate has a way of making you feel like an animal, a beast with fire in your eyes. I could feel that as my hate for the view out the window grew. Today as I got up from lying for hours, I looked out the window, I saw that house, and I lost it. I screamed at the house, I clawed at the window, and I growled at the view.

The growl probably did it. The scream and the claw were maybe ok, normal human reactions to isolation. But, the growl, the growl, was telling me something needed to change. I needed to do something new if I was going to survive as a ghost and not transform into something more sinister that I felt trying to claw through my soul.

I turned and sat in the corner of the bedroom. This was

not a particularly good place to sit, but I chose it because it was simply somewhere I hadn't sat before. I looked at the small room where I spent so much of my time when I was living. The room and home felt like it was ours. My parents were also dead, and I was technically under the care of my aunt. She lived with her boyfriend and never thought about where I lived or what I did, so although I rented a room from a stranger, I spent most of my time here in this room.

I looked at our bed. Ash rolled up in our flannel sheets like he was trapped there. Occasionally, he would roll over a bit more; every few hours, I heard sobbing from the blankets, and twice I saw his arms stretch out from them before they wrapped themselves back into his bleak cocoon.

I looked at Ash's Marvel posters, one on each wall, that I planned to frame as a sweet surprise one day. These were the stolen memories that I would never get to make. All the times I told myself one day, now thrown into the wind to return as nevers. The most difficult part about memories never had is that they forever gnaw at you. I hoped we were reincarnated and that, over time, we got to experience all the things we could ever imagine. But the ghost version of myself who sat in the corner of Ash's room had a pretty good feeling I was wrong, and all I really had was the memories I already made.

Like the memory of the faded white dresser and nightstands in the bedroom, I remembered Ash, and I dug into our box where we saved our money. We were going to make our first adult purchase. We had stacks of clothes on the floor of the room and never felt like anything was clean. We weren't going to do something adult like buying furniture without also having fun. What is the point of even being an adult if you don't enjoy it?

We took some Vodka from his mother's room and drank up a storm before we had Alan drive us to make the purchase. We got them from a local thrift store for cheap because, in my drunken state, I was also more friendly. I walked in and pretended to recognize the employee. I asked about his mother and told him that the playground we used to play at was torn down. He seemed confused but still enjoyed the attention and gave us the furniture for half of the 100 dollars the store had asked for. When we got home, Ash took a knife and carved a heart with our initials into both the dresser and nightstand. I could see the wobbly heart from where I sat and just wanted to live through those stupid little moments once more.

You only have one option when you can't make any new memories. You can take time and space to remember and study previous ones. For others, spending some time remembering your life could bring joy and spare them from boredom, but I was searching for answers.

2

Love

Ash and I met during our Junior year of high school. I was a bit of an outcast amongst the typical students, which I adopted from my rocker parents before they passed. I also developed a general feeling of animosity and angst towards the rest of society. It wasn't that I thought the world was a bad place full of bad people. I just wasn't that interested in discovering who was good and who wasn't. So, instead, I mostly kept to myself to prevent any confusion.

I didn't care what other people thought, or at least that's what I tried to tell myself. Really, I hoped that people would think that I didn't care what they thought. I wore torn shirts and pants every day, partially because I didn't have money for new clothes, but partly because it was the look I wanted.

My hair, well, my hair was the dead give-away of wanting to not blend in with the sheep. It was pitch black, and I cut it myself, which was evident by the uneven layers. I decided that the look I was going for was wild, and my hair abided. My curls went in every which direction like they were all trying to run away. This was not a looking for love hairstyle, and I was not a looking for love girl. So, when Ash broke my world to pieces, I was utterly unprepared.

That world I once knew all came tumbling down for the second time, in November of my Junior year. I walked into my Physics class, expecting a typical day. My Physics teacher, Mr. Alex, stood in a worn-down suit at the door and greeted us as we entered. I ignored him and kept my head down as usual. I didn't want to be mean to people, but I didn't want to be noticed either. So, I would overthink the impact of me ignoring people like this but never be brave enough to change it. I tunneled to the back corner of the classroom.

The classroom always felt quietly dreadful. It had one tiny window on the wall. The window looked out of place from the unintentionally grey concrete surrounding it. It also seemed like the saddest little gesture to show we were human beings in this classroom. Here, have a tiny and gross window; that's all humans need, right? I didn't find any comfort in it at all.

I pulled out my notebook, pencil, and book, which I liked to read whenever the teacher wasn't paying attention. I watched my classmates walk in and fill the room, judging each one as they entered. It was a terrible habit that I didn't get the chance to fix before I died. Reflecting now, I think my instinct to judge others came from thinking that others were always judging me too. Regardless, I did it every day. I thought about how that girl wore too much makeup, that boy was trying too hard, and that other boy wasn't trying hard enough. It was a dirty game that made me feel dirty from the inside out.

I was disappointed by yet another typical Tuesday. But

that's the thing you never know when a typical day will become a crucial day. That's when Ash walked in. I noticed he was new and quickly allowed myself to appreciate how incredibly good looking he was. Then my breathing paused as we briefly locked eyes. I immediately averted my eyes and opened my book. He walked straight to the permanently open seat right next to me.

My thoughts about his appearance had quickly dissolved into pure anxiety and anger. I could not risk someone sitting next to me or, worse, someone talking to me. I worked so hard to establish this permanent look on my face that accurately communicated that people should stay away from me. But he didn't stay away from me, to say the least. Instead, he pulled out the chair and sat down next to me like it had happened every day for a century.

His presence that first day felt like a rock was placed on my chest. I couldn't move. I couldn't breathe. I could still give him a dirty look the few times I accidentally locked eyes with him. It was the most uncomfortable I felt in a long time. I was so used to people not calling my bluff, leaving me alone because I seemed strong and angry. They were right that I was angry. But I felt anything but strong, and his presence so close to me made me even weaker.

Every day after that, I moved my seat. If my stare wouldn't scare him away, I could run away. But every day, he came and sat by me no matter where I sat. I stared at him one day when he fell asleep in class. It was the only time I could get an in-depth look without him noticing. He had this light brown hair that shined. It was so golden, and I almost wanted to check for glitter but knew I only had a precious few moments to memorize him.

Everything else about him was dark, his dark t-shirt and pants laying across his deep brown skin. He had this long body that slumped over the entire desk as he slept. The bell rang, and I physically jumped; I felt immediately ashamed and as if I had been busted. But he didn't seem to notice at all and grabbed his bag quickly by instinct, and went for the doors.

Ash never spoke to me in that class. He usually smirked as he sat next to me day after day as if he knew how uncomfortable he made me. I hated that smirk. It made me want to punch him. But, as extremely confrontational as my dirty looks were, I didn't have the body to match it.

One day I went into that class with a different plan in mind. I saw an open seat between two students. One was a nerdy girl that always wore the same bright pink bow in her braided hair, and the other a popular girl who resembled Barbie, who didn't catch an open seat with her friends today. Which, for her, was probably absolutely devastating. Barbie and I went to school together since Elementary. She was never kind to me and never particularly interesting.

This would be the single bravest thing I had possibly ever done. I sat down in between the two students, who both looked at me from the corner of their eyes nervously. I stumped the handsome Ash. He walked in, looked at me. For the first time, I looked right back up at him as well, and I smirked. The power of that revenge smirk rushed through my veins.

With more confidence than what I ever had in my life, Ash walked up to the blonde Barbie to my right.

"Excuse me."

I spent almost every day in class with this girl, and let me tell you, I never heard her voice go this high in my life.

"Hey! I've been hoping you would introduce yourself. I'm Daisy."

I thought; finally, I lost him. May he and Barbie live together forever and happily.

"Oh, no, I wasn't introducing myself. I was wondering if you would move to that seat back there, so I could have this one."

Barbie looked so confused and ready to cry. Just then, maybe before a tear of rejection had flowed down, he pulled five bucks out of his back pocket and motioned it to her. She got up with the funniest little scowl I'd ever seen. She looked Ash up and down and walked to a new seat without taking the money. Ash flung his backpack down, smirked at me larger than usual, and sat down in the seat beside me.

This went on all school year. After about a month, I stopped trying to avoid it, stopped trying to come early to get a new seat, and stopped letting it ruin my day. I expected him to sit down next to me every day.

I only saw him outside of school once. I walked home from the grocery store when I saw him standing in front of the mall with some of his friends. He was sitting up on a small wall and listening to a pretty girl who wasn't from our school. I stopped in my tracks when I saw I would have to walk past him. I could take the long way around the parking lot, but now I was contemplating whether avoiding this cute boy was worth an extra 30 minutes of walking.

I set down the groceries, zipped up my black hoodie, and put my hood up. I was worried about what I would make for dinner, and I needed to do some laundry. I didn't have time to be concerned about some boy. So, I took a deep breath and started to walk past the group of teens. I was terrified knowing that he would stop everything and make everyone look at me. I walked by and didn't hear a word from him. The girl continued with a fake story about getting arrested, and my walk was undisturbed.

I felt like a fish that successfully swum right by a group of sharks. But I also couldn't help but be curious. So, I turned around just after I passed them and looked up from under my hood. Sure enough, I immediately locked eyes with Ash. It was in those eyes, and at that moment that I knew he would ruin my life or save it.

We never talked about that moment till much later. Instead, we sat beside each other, in silence, day after day. Sometimes it seemed to me his chair was just a bit closer to mine. Then others it seemed farther apart. There were days when he got a text, and I would feel a bit jealous, but never enough to say a word. Other days I felt so comfortable that it was like he wasn't even there.

On the last day of school before summer, he actually wasn't there. I looked at the empty seat next to me suddenly with a feeling of deep and terrible longing. I found that I had grown to appreciate his presence. Every time the door opened during that class, I looked at it with hope, but it was never him. The class felt like it lasted for three years. I couldn't believe it, all this time being uncomfortable, creeped out, and angry, and yet I could barely stand to be without him in class anymore.

Once the bell finally rang, I let everyone else leave first, then threw my books in my bag. As I walked out the door, I turned around to look back at the classroom. The classroom I would probably never be in again. The class I met that strange boy Ash in, who I would probably never see again either.

Right as I had this thought, my body, that was headed out the door without my eyes or attention, suddenly and violently ran into something. I fell backward, and a hand grabbed me by the arm and kept me up, Ash.

"Thinking about me, Sita?"

I said what I always said to him, nothing. I walked past him, almost shoving by to get outside. Then I rushed as quickly as I could through the hallway. It was eerily, quiet, and empty. I shuffled, trying to move fast. It was difficult, though, because a part of me knew he might still be looking at me. So, I was also trying to look cute as I walked. Small moments like this reminded me my walls weren't as strong as I'd built them to be.

My stall in the classroom at least gave time for the parade of students to have already made their way outside. Which was a welcome relief because while others felt comfort in large crowds, I always felt uncomfortable. I much preferred the empty halls where the joy had already passed. What remained looked like Hansel and Gretel had left the building; instead of breadcrumbs, the students had left trash, paper, and binders in their path. I picked up trash on my way out the door and had stuffed it all into my black canvas bag to throw out later.

I stopped once I got outside, wondering what I might do now that school was out. There was a rush of students stripping off their hoodies and sweats to reveal small summer clothing. A group of girls was piling into a white Jeep. There was an extra girl on every girl's lap, and they were all screaming as the driver blasted music. I recognized one of them as Anna, a girl I lived next door to growing up. I hadn't talked to her since my parents passing, and when she had tried to call, I blocked her number.

I saw a group of both girls and boys wrestling in the grass. Some of them kissed, while others, who were probably less adept at social cues, were actually hurting each other. Another group was skateboarding in the parking lot, lighting off small little fireworks. All of them, celebrating and experiencing joy and bond I had yet to experience myself.

I thought about how I should celebrate, another year surviving being around all this false energy. But I didn't have much of a choice. I spent most of these 11 years doing everything I could to push people away. I didn't trust them, and I just didn't see why everyone needed each other so much. It felt so pathetic to me, their constant reliance on each other. But now, as I stood there staring at their joy, I wondered who was actually the pathetic one. Then I felt a tap on my shoulder, Ash again.

"Let's go celebrate, I know of a place, it's a cool little Mexican restaurant, and my cousin will give us a beer if we buy food."

I still remembered the feeling of his hand on my shoulder

when he tapped me. The energy he left there made me feel like I was floating and grounded at the same time. This guy was not going to let up. He was probably going to follow me for the rest of my life. Little did I know then, it would actually be the other way around. But the reality is, I wanted to celebrate. I wanted to talk to someone. I even wanted a fuckin beer. So, for the first time in my life, I said yes. Well, not literally. I just shrugged, and when he started walking, I followed.

3

Sign

I don't sleep. Ever since I died, I can't. Sometimes I lay down in bed next to Ash, but nothing happens. I just stare at him until there's nothing left to stare at, and then I stare at the ceiling. Ash is the opposite. Since I died, all he did was sleep. I hadn't seen him leave the house since he had to go get toilet paper a while ago. When he did wake up, he used the restroom, sometimes got some water, and then rolled back into bed.

He became a pathetic version of the man I fell in love with. I wondered if I would have been the same if he had died. I couldn't imagine living without him, and at least now, I still had him here. But he didn't have me at all. I ruined his life by dying; of all the ways I could have destroyed his life, this one was the worst. I stared at that golden hair and wondered what I could possibly do differently, how I could possibly save him. I always came up with nothing, nothing other than watching him and mourning with him.

But today was different; around 2:00 pm, there was a banging on the front door. I was lying next to Ash, staring at the black tv. The banging got louder and shook the room. I watched him roll over, ignoring it. I went downstairs and tried to look through the peephole since Ash wasn't of much help.

My body didn't exactly work like it used to. I didn't have feet; I just kind of hovered. But I hovered at the height I died at, which was a whopping 5'1. Without feet, I couldn't look at anything taller than me, including through the peephole. The banging continued with a panic-like tone. I went to the window and tried to move the curtain back.

When I was alive, I often watched scary movies and ghost hunters. I always wondered why ghosts never showed themselves more. The reality was, I couldn't. I had been trying to send a sign to Ash since I came here. Now, I wanted to see who was outside to see if he was in danger, but my hand just swiped right through the curtain.

As I tried to nudge the curtain, I turned around and saw Ash coming down the stairs. He was pulling on a dirty brown robe that I hated but could never get him to donate. He bought that robe for himself when he got his first job. It was a comfort to him more than a cover. He pulled his hand through his hair as if to fix it, but the grease made it look terrible regardless.

The banging was now so loud I couldn't help but be scared. I wanted someone to hold me. On the other hand, Ash didn't hesitate, didn't see who it was, and just opened the door. I was relieved to see it was his mother at the door. Her grey hair puffed out slightly, and she wore a too-tight polka-dot dress.

She held two large bags of leftovers from a local diner. When Ash opened the door, she smiled at him just a moment, then pushed past him and walked right through me. She stopped after she did that.

"It's so cold in here, Ash. Do you have the heat on?"

This was actually Theresa's home. She had her name on the documents and had a room. But most of the time, she wasn't there. While I was thinking about college and dreams, Ash was busy thinking about bills and food. It didn't come as a surprise that she had come violently knocking. So far, she lost 17 house keys. Ash stopped making her new copies, and she stopped asking. He only felt relieved that she didn't bring her on again off again boyfriend, Tony, this time. Who had terribly dyed pitch-black hair and always somehow managed to be even drunker than Theresa.

This wasn't a step up from my own mother. My parents were very sweet and affectionate when I was younger. They were the perfect couple and perfect parents. I never once saw them fight, never once felt unloved. I wish I appreciated that when I had the opportunity.

I began regretting it when both my parents died when I was only 14 years old. The only place for me to go was with my aunt. My aunt was young and not interested in having children. She told me she would adopt me, but I would be on my own. Which wasn't too long before Ash and I started raising ourselves together.

Ash rubbed his eyes and didn't respond to her question about the cold, which didn't seem to affect her at all. She just kept walking towards the small kitchen at the duplex's back, with Ash following behind. But, as he walked by me, he stopped too. I went as close to him as possible. I tried to put my hand on his face. He stared into the nothing. I wondered if he could feel me, for the first time if he knew I was here. That moment, that brief moment when he paused by me, was the most alive I felt since before I died. But, before I knew it, he had moved on.

Even though Ash had paused by me for a moment, I don't think his mother had stopped talking. When we walked into the kitchen, she was mid-sentence.

"And so, I told her that it wasn't like that, that you are so young. Your friends left this in the mailbox." She said, turning and placing a new phone on the counter. Ash grabbed it and took a seat on a stool. He immediately started to transfer his old broken phone to this one, with an urgency like maybe I would call. His mother began to pull a half-eaten cheeseburger and fries from the bag and placed them on bright red plastic plates. Then, the strangest thing happened, out of the corner of my eye, I saw someone.

Someone was sitting in the corner of the kitchen, an old man, almost see-through. He was crouched down and outlining the traces of our tile with his hands. At first, I found myself frightened. I always believed in ghosts but never wanted to see one. It was just one of those things I knew but never felt a desire to feel. I quickly realized that my fear of ghosts was now only terribly ironic and yet made complete sense. I have always been slightly frightened of myself in one way or another.

I tried something I had tried every day with Ash without success. I spoke.

"Excuse me."

He didn't look up, so I went over closer and knelt down.

"Sir?"

He looked up, leading with his white beard and stern brown eyes.

"Look, lady, I'm not trying to start anything. I can't help it; my soul is attached to her." He said, pointing towards Ash's mother, Theresa.

"Please don't hurt me. I won't cause any trouble at all, I promise. I just have to protect my grandbaby."

"You can hear me? You can see me?"

He looked up with concern and quickly dropped his stern face for a kinder one. He stood up from the floor and took my face in his hands. I didn't feel it, but I saw it.

"Sita?"

"Yes! Yes! I'm Sita. Do I know you?"

"Oh, no baby, but I've been following my grandbaby around since I died. I've seen you before, with my boy Ash. Oh no, this is why she has been so distraught and worried. I didn't know you had passed."

I turned to see Ash reluctantly eating his food. I felt he was safe enough that maybe I could worry about myself, and you know, ask some questions about being trapped as a ghost forever, which I wasn't particularly thrilled about.

"How long have you been here?" the sweet old man asked.

"I don't really know."

"And you're attached to Ash?"

"I think so. A couple days ago, I tried to leave. I couldn't move from the house, though. Another day, when Ash went to the store, I was able to leave with him."

"Yes, yes, you're attached to Ash, as I am attached to his

mother. I am waiting. I am happy to watch her grow, even though it's not what I pictured."

"Do you have a choice?"

"No. I was killed during a fight. At first, people cared, but after a short while of them not knowing who actually shot me, they stopped looking. I am happy. I wouldn't want to be without Theresa, no matter how turbulent she is. So, I'll wait for her to pass, then I'll be free to go where I please."

"What if they had found your killer?"

"Then I would haunt him instead. That's how it works. I can guard my grandbaby only because I don't know my killer."

I looked back towards Ash. "So, I will guard Ash until I can haunt my killer?"

"That's right, Sita. If, though, if you can haunt your killer. It is stupendously difficult for a ghost to solve a murder without the help of a human. Unfortunately, just like when you were living, it is also hard to find a human who can really listen."

"And what about when he passes?"

"When he passes, you can go wherever you want. You can be whatever you want."

"And what if what I want is to not be a ghost?"

Theresa began grabbing her oversized purse and started making her way out the door. As he left with her, he responded with a chuckle,

"Then just don't get murdered in the first place."

Ash's mother left; Ash took back off his filthy robe and curled back into bed to sleep once again. He slept with my favorite cardigan—a green plaid one, which he cuddled up with like a stuffed animal each night and day. The next day was one of the bad days, which always had a way of making me miss the sleepy days. The phone rang around 9 am, and it was his work calling again. I hadn't seen him go to work since I passed. He threw the phone across the room. He rolled over to face my side of the bed.

The phone just didn't seem to be stopping this time. I slowly laid down where he was looking and told myself he was looking right at me. Then his arm came down and went right through me, as he hit the bed. He rolled out of bed on the other side and just collapsed. I rushed over to his side. He was crying, weeping, and hitting the floor over and over.

He continued to move through me as I continued to try to hold him, and he kept moving aggressively. For a moment, I felt frustrated with him, angry that it was all about him. I was in pain too.

Then he began to speak through sobs.

"Why?!! Why would you do this to me? How could you leave me, Sita?"

I was responding in a panic, shouting in the hopes he would be able to hear me.

"I didn't! I'm right here, Ash! You're all I have!"

He calmed his sobs.

"Sita, are you here? Please, please, Sita, if you're here, show me, do something, move something, send me a sign."

I stood up with a mission in mind. We would both find peace if he knew I was here. I did everything I could. I shook our white and flimsy bed. I tried to throw the months of dirty clothes he had lying around. I tore at the Marvel posters. I pounded on the wall and punched the large mirror in the corner again and again. But nothing, nothing moved, nothing made a noise.

Have you ever been so frustrated you just needed to hit something? I understood why ghosts were so angry. I understood that anger just sits in your soul with a heavy and all-consuming weight that must be released, or it will weigh you down altogether.

I collapsed next to Ash after my tantrum after I tried everything in my power to show him that I was there. He looked around, seemingly for the sign I couldn't deliver. He wiped his face, sighed, and said aloud, but not to me this time, "I know she isn't here. I'm being stupid." and with those words that stabbed me like a knife, he sluggishly moved back towards the bed. He curled back into the fetal position with my cardigan wrapped up in his arms and fell back asleep.

A few days later, it was my funeral. I only knew this because of my new favorite hobby of eavesdropping on Ash's conversations. When I was younger, I used to imagine my funeral. When I was young and still lived with my parents and still had friends, I would imagine them all mourning me and regretting every wrong thing they ever did to me.

The older I got, the less I pictured it. When I knew more people and didn't like any of them, I knew I liked to think about their pain. But once I had Ash, I didn't imagine it anymore because his pain felt too much to bear. Besides, I couldn't picture people actually showing up anyway.

Ash took a shower, and I watched, jealous of the water. As he got ready in his black button-up shirt and black slacks, I realized I had no idea what we were going to. Based on phone calls, it seemed that Alan had done most of the planning. I knew it wasn't a traditional funeral, they had talked about me not wanting that, and they were right.

We got in the car, and he silently cried the whole way. He arrived at a funeral home hidden in trees. Ash went in, and a woman with a brown bun and a tight pencil dress greeted him when he entered through the front door.

"Hello, how can I help you?" She said in a tight voice.

"I'm here to pick up an urn for a funeral."

"I need your ID and name of the deceased."

He handed her his ID and then paused uncomfortably, until finally, "Sita Gonzalez."

"Great, we have that ready for you. Take a seat. I will be right out."

There was a central waiting room surrounded by doors. The furniture and décor felt like it was stuck in time from the 1970s. I felt death in the air. Ash sat and stared in one direction like the half-human I had watched him become. I sat next to him and stared in the same direction, matching his sense of loss. There was a picture between the two doors across from us, a family in all-black attire.

The photo looked like it was taken out front. Only two of the maybe ten people were smiling. Only three of the ten looked like they had been crying. The rest of the family wore sunglasses and large hats, disguising their true feelings to the world.

While I studied the picture, out of the corner of my eye, I saw someone. I looked over the door to our right. I saw a large man with long brown hair peering at us halfway through the door. But he wasn't like the other ghost I met. He had a black outline around him. When my eyes met his, I felt cold all over, and fear ran through me.

I pulled in my legs onto the couch and sunk in deeper to it. I hid behind Ash and tried not to look at the man again. I dug my head into my knees and prayed that it would end soon because something felt horribly wrong. I prayed the tight woman would come back out with my body. But instead, I felt a rush of wind push me back into the couch.

I jumped and looked up above my legs. The man with the long hair was standing right in front of me. His eyes felt like they were looking inside of me. He moved in so close to my face there was only a thin piece of air separating us. I instinctively pulled back and held onto Ash as if he could protect me. I was frozen. The man hissed, and I jumped back.

When I did that, he slowly turned his head and focused on Ash. He moved over towards Ash, and I pulled at Ash's jacket. I was now pushing him in the opposite direction than I originally was. The man pulled his hand up and slowly reached out to touch Ash's face.

"Stay away from him," I said in a voice just barely over a whisper.

He looked at me but didn't move. Then he was looking back at Ash again. He smirked, and just then, the woman came back out with the urn. Out of habit, I took a breath of relief. Ash slowly took the urn into his hands. It all felt like I was watching it in slow motion. It was a golden urn with a leaf painted on the side in maroon. It shined and somehow made me feel a bit of peace. Like it was really over, I was really dead, and my body was gone. A terrible reality, but I felt grateful for the finality of it all.

I was quickly pulled back to the man staring into Ash as he took the urn. That's what actually makes life so hard and terrible. That life goes on no matter what you need. I needed a moment with my death. I needed a moment to process my own body being here. But instead, I had to stop and wonder what I was going to do about this creepy man that looked like he might murder my boyfriend.

We turned, and Ash slowly walked to the door with his eyes fixed on the urn. The man was following us with his eyes fixed on Ash. I moved back towards the man and put my hand out to touch him and stop him. My hand went right through him. His eyebrows curved in, and he grabbed my wrist. The strange thing was that I could feel it. It was the most human I felt since I had died. I looked at my wrist in his hands and looked back to him, more scared than ever. This man was not a ghost like me; he was something different. But, strangely, it also felt nice to be touched again. Ash was out the door, and I was back next to him, looking back at the man who smiled at us both.

Ash set the urn in the front seat where I usually sat and buckled it in. So, I moved into the back seat. I was more myself than my body. But here I was riding back seat to ashes who would never speak or think again. We drove in silence to a small park that I had never been to before.

It was open and large, with few people in it. There was a total of four blue balloons awkwardly blowing in the wind. A single white plastic table was set up with half a dozen roses sitting on top and three pictures of myself and Ash on the table. I peered out and observed the scene.

I imagined my funeral would not be big but average. I

imagined people would be devastated. I imagined elaborate flowers and a slide show. I imagined everyone I ever met being there. But I suddenly realized that as I looked out at what looked like the saddest birthday in the world, that's not what I earned. Ash mumbled to himself a "Fuck" and then took the urn into his hands. He looked up to no one and said, "Sorry, honey." I appreciated the sentiment.

We took an artificial breath together and left the car. He walked straight to the white table and set the urn down. He brushed his hand across it, and I tried to imagine it was me. He pulled up one of the only chairs and sat next to the urn. My aunt walked over to where he sat and stood over him.

She looked like she was doing well without the burden of me. I wondered for a moment if this felt like even more of a relief to her. Now she really didn't have any responsibility towards me. Her short curly blonde hair was perfectly maintained, and she had almost no makeup on but still looked perfect.

"Ash, I'm sorry for your loss."

Ash didn't bother to respond. I loved him more at that moment. I did look to her, though. I recognized a small piece of my mother in her eyes. It was then I realized that my entire family was dead. Now my aunt didn't have any family. I felt bad for her for a moment before realizing that she gave me that reality when I wasn't even ready for it. She was my only family, and she simply threw me away. She walked away after the small meaningless comment and straight to her car in the parking lot. As she drove away, I felt relieved that this terrible funeral was now just a little less awful.

Next on the bad family members acting caring show was

good old Theresa. She pulled her tight yellow dress down. She walked towards Ash. But she stopped when she saw my English teacher standing there. He was a middle-aged man with a beard and worn-down outfit. She stopped to say something flirty and then continued towards us. Her boyfriend, Tony, was standing at the back in a leather jacket and jeans with stains all over. He didn't notice Theresa's flirting because he was too busy chugging from his flask. She awkwardly put her hand on Ash. She at least knelt to his level, although I had suspicions, she had only done this so she could bend over in front of my English teacher. She looked into Ash's eyes and gently pulled his head up to look at her.

"Ash baby, do you want to say a few words? I think we all want to get out of here, and maybe if you say something, we will feel more comfortable leaving."

That day was exhausting, and all any of us wanted to do was leave.

Ash stood up as his mom slowly stood up too, looking back and winking at my English Teacher.

"Thank you all for coming today."

I saw Theresa, my English teacher, Anna, the girl I went to elementary with, Alan and two of his friends, and two coworkers. That was it. That was the number of people who cared about me enough to come to my funeral.

"I know that Sita would really appreciate you all being here." He stared past all of them into the grass behind them, and his eyes began to tear up.

"Sita was my everything. I would do anything for her."

"*Then, see me,*" I said, standing right in front of him, slowly waving my hand.

"Now that she is gone. Nothing matters."

"I'm not gone."

Then he turned toward the table and picked up my urn and walked back to the car. Everyone awkwardly looked at each other and completed sullen head nods, and they all went off in different directions. It was the perfect ending to the most imperfect funeral there had ever been. Ash held water in his eyes and drove with an unwarranted amount of determination. Then all at once and without warning, I couldn't stop laughing.

Of course, there were moments I felt that that sad funeral was tragic and deserved. But, for a moment, I remembered exactly who I was. Society told me I needed people to care about me and treat me a certain way. Society told me that a fuller funeral meant I was a better person. But how good of a person can you really be if it relies on what other people think about you rather than who you really are?

4

Orphan

It can be difficult to be anti-social in a world that seems to run on your ability to be social. People were always pulling at me to be my friend or enemy when I was alive. So, it was actually quite the accomplishment to have such a small and sad funeral. This wasn't an accomplishment I would have wanted at one time.

I actually had a pretty normal childhood that didn't hint to all my tragic endings. When I was a little girl, I thought the world was a bright place tainted only by grumpy old adults. My mom and dad raised me to be kind, that other people's opinions weren't important, and I believed them. Unfortunately, no happy kid really makes it through middle school, unscarred and unchanged.

When I was twelve, I was drowning in the evil hell that was middle school girl drama. I still remembered my fight with a girl named Liza because she told me once that my hair looked like a bird's nest. That stupid comment haunted me at night, and I spent many long showers thinking about what

I should have said as a comeback. Eventually, things calmed, and by the time I was thirteen, my focus had shifted.

At thirteen years old, I thought that Cale was the best thing to happen to the world. He was a sleek "poet" with slick brown hair. I put poet in quotes because he had written one poem. But in my eyes as a kid, that was enough to make him William Shakespeare. My biggest stress was that he said he liked me but kissed another girl at recess. Devastating. I can honestly say that was one of the hardest things to deal with, even now as the ghost of a murdered orphan girl.

When I was fourteen, I had friends that I thought I would never lose. I had a boy I thought I would always love. I had everything that came with being a teen, ready to burst out and be an adult. I didn't know then that being an adult was coming much faster than I could have ever prepared for. It was all waiting for me on the other side of that last dinner.

My dad had this long grey beard and had combed his brown hair back. He was wearing a sweater, which he always looked weird in. He usually danced and sang around the house without a shirt and in some torn jeans. But he looked nicer than usual because he'd gone to a job interview that day. He sold his art online but recently had seen a drop in sales and searched for a job for some extra income.

"I don't know. I think it went very well." He said as he shoveled spaghetti into his mouth.

He could have said relatively anything, and my mom would have been supportive. She was already smiling her large smile that I was always envious of. She quickly braided her long dark hair before responding, "I'm so proud of you, baby." She turned to me.

"Sita, how was school today?"

The worst time that you can lose a parent is as a teen. Something comes in our "How to be a Teen" handbook that just makes us not appreciate our parents as much as we should. My mother asking this simple question of how school was today drove me a little crazy. They couldn't understand my problems, and to be honest, I didn't understand theirs. But I loved and appreciated them enough to not be rude, at least.

"It was fine, mom."

My dad laughed, "Well, don't divulge too much information. Anyway, I think I'll head to a concert tonight. My buddy Dale is playing down the road at the bar."

I knew my mother would again support what my dad wanted to do. I'd heard at school about kids who grew up in bad homes. One girl in my art class once told the entire class that her mother left her father for her sister's friend. She said they yelled at each other every night before it happened and that she was very happy they wouldn't be together anymore. My home life couldn't have been any different. My mother and father were so in love, so supportive and kind to each other that it made me feel like the odd one out sometimes.

"Well, that sounds great." My mom responded, then she looked at me again with expectation in her eyes.

"Cool, Dad. I think I'll just do some homework tonight. I was hoping to get enough done that I could go to Kayla's sleepover this weekend."

My mother smiled, proud of me for getting out a full sentence. "Well, that sounds great too, Sita."

This was our last conversation. It was also the beginning of me giving up on society. It was something about the fakeness of that final conversation. Why couldn't we have been deeper? Why couldn't I have expressed who I was and how I felt?

That night I woke up to the sound of my mother's scream. A scream that reached into my body and pulled it inside out, it was paralyzing. So much so that it took a few minutes for me to get out of the safety of my bed. But I rolled out in my large Disney World shirt and with my curls in a secure bun on my head. I slowly opened my door and walked to the landing to look down and see my mother.

She had the phone in her hand, tears in rivers, and was now only screaming every couple of moments. I took the first step down the stairs. But before I could step on the second stair, she was grabbing the car keys by the door. Before I could take the third stair, she was out the door.

She just left me. My first thought was my dad; nothing would upset my mother that much unless it was my dad. So, I sat on the step for two hours, wondering whether my father was dead or alive. After two hours, I moved back to my bed. I didn't know where my mom went, and her phone was turned off. I didn't have anyone's number who might know. So, I just laid there until the sun came up, images of every worst-case scenario flashing through my mind.

When the sun did come up, my mother returned. But she never really returned. She came into my room and sat on my bed. Her eyes were glazed over, and she didn't look at me. She pulled down at her flowy purple skirt, and I noticed that she made it messier than it had been before. She smelled like cigarettes and something strong that I couldn't quite identify. She took a deep breath, pulled some sort of pill out of her purse, and took it right in front of me. Then she closed her eyes.

"Mom?"

She shook and opened her eyes.

"Your dad is dead."

Tears began to roll down her face, and she pulled out another pill. I wondered if I should stop her. But I had it in my head that adults just must know always to do the right thing.

"Car accident."

"That isn't true," I said, stuttering a bit.

She started to gaze off into the corner of the room. "Sita, you must know that..." Then she began to fall asleep. I had never seen anything like it. Her eyelids fell on each other, and her body collapsed. I caught her and shook her, "Mom! Mom!" She sat back up and shook all over like she vibrated.

"Sorry, Sita, long night."

"Maybe you should go to bed, mom."

I laid back down and tried to sleep myself while also trying to process what just happened. There were bursts of realization that my dad was actually gone, and I would cry silent tears and scream into my pillow. This was followed by shots of numbness that made it feel like nothing in the world was real. I finally got up the next day. Around noon I drank some water and filled a glass for my mother. I slowly opened her door to walk in.

I knew she was dead the moment I saw her. She was spread out on the bed with vomit beside her mouth, and her purse with the pill bottles all fallen out. Just like that, the concert lead to a bed that lead to me being an orphan.

For hours at the hospital, a nurse kept an eye on me while

also watching a beauty YouTube video. Until finally, my aunt came to pick me up. Her hair was longer then, and she looked young in her workout gear and ponytail. Her first words came with a glimpse of what lay ahead for me.

"Please get in the car already, Sita. I had to drive 30 minutes to get here."

That was the beginning of another year of my aunt treating me like I was born with the sole intention of ruining her life. She would list day after day all the ways I was an inconvenience for her. A couple of weeks after my parents died, I brought up how I really should be going to school. She snapped and said that she was providing everything for me, and I wasn't appreciative enough. I explained I would call and find a bus and walk to it every day so she wouldn't have to do anything. She complained and said that I shouldn't have told her all this because I was old enough to make these choices myself.

I tried my best to be more convenient just so I had somewhere to stay. I worried that each time I spoke, and each time I moved, she was closer to throwing me out on to the street. I tried to stay invisible and not even be home when she was. But as if I took a piece of her soul each time I took a breath, she was fumbling to find a way out, so she called the lawyers.

When I turned eighteen, I would be allowed to have my parent's inheritance. Until then, my aunt was in charge. If my aunt was allowed to spend it herself, I am beyond positive she would have spent every dine. Fortunately, she couldn't touch it.

Eventually, when she would tell me she would lend me some of my inheritance to leave, I stopped trying to please her. I took the money she offered and rented a room that didn't ask any questions about my age.

Sometimes I did think about my aunt and whether a bad family was better than no family. But I tried to remember that if someone doesn't want you, you can't make them. The irony is that the only person I wanted to be close to didn't want anything to do with me. She must have the inheritance herself, now that I died. It made me wonder whether that made her like me more than she had when I was alive.

But this question, like so many more, would remain unanswered. I think unanswered questions were part of why my aunt hated me so much. I didn't know at the time the consequences that came with just telling the truth. I told the police about the pills and the falling asleep when my mother got home. What I didn't know, and they didn't know, was whether or not she was dying right in front of me. It was too close to determine. Did I kill my mother by sending her to bed?

When you have problems like this as a then fifteen-year-old, all your other problems become silly. I didn't care whether boys liked me or girls wanted to be me anymore. While my friends were contemplating which dress was best for homecoming, I considered whether you could go to hell for unintentional murder.

5

Graduation

I dreamt of my graduation for many years, the way other girls dreamt of their wedding day. I always thought it was supposed to be when real adulthood hit. People try to trick you into not looking up to being an adult. They will tell you how terribly difficult and exhausting it is. But that's what I wanted. I wanted to be able to choose who I was.

Every day I worried about who was going to be in control of me next. Would the state find me and send me to foster care? Would my aunt actually want me at home? Would Ash want me to live a certain way? Would a teacher tell me I couldn't graduate? Would they send me to juvie? I pictured graduation as the day that would change everything, where my life would finally start being the result of my own choices, actions, and decisions.

Instead, I was trapped in a ghost-like world that was not the result of any of those things, where I had no idea how to control or come out of it. I was more trapped than I had been when I was living.

I was standing downstairs in the kitchen, staring at the graduation invite that I taped to the fridge. I knew Theresa and her boyfriend wouldn't go, but I didn't want Ash and me to ever forget. It just felt normal, as if I had lived in a normal world with my normal family, with my normal graduation invite on the fridge.

I traced the invite's royal blue side into a square and tried to touch the engraved words. I stared for a while. I wanted to pretend I was there and that I'd done it, I'd escaped. I waited, wondering whether or not Ash would attend graduation at all. I understood why he wouldn't want to. If the tables were turned, I doubted that I would be attending. It was a formality unless you had someone to make proud.

Ash slept and slept, blissfully unaware that if he didn't attend the graduation, it meant that I couldn't either. I highly suggest if someone close to you ever dies, you experience as much as you can. They could be relying on you; they could be bored as fuck.

Finally, I stopped staring at the invite and switched to the clock. It was noon; the ceremony was at 1:30 pm. I remembered those who were graduating were supposed to arrive by now for a quick rehearsal first. I don't know why I wanted to see the graduation so much. It didn't mean anything for me now. I couldn't picture anything in my dead life that would require a diploma.

Something made me want to accomplish one last thing, though, to know that I actually did something. I went upstairs and found Ash wrapped up in the blankets with his mouth open a bit. I tried to tug at the blankets. His phone started ringing and didn't stop.

"*Come on, Ash. That's probably your friends. I want to go, Ash.*" I said while trying to hit the bed to make it move. I jumped back because, at the same time, Ash moved with a grunt. He wrapped the blanket in his hand and aggressively rubbed his eyes. Somehow, I think I turned on the lights. That woke him immediately, and he sat straight up in fear.

He looked at his phone and saw Alan and put it on the speaker while he got up and put on some clothes.

"Hello"

"Hey, man!" Alan said, sounding relieved and also unprepared. He continued, "I just haven't heard from you in so long." Ash didn't respond as he looked on the room's floor to try to decide which dirty t-shirt might be the least dirty. Alan only gave a moment before continuing, "Anyway, lots of people are wondering if you're coming today. Will you be there, man?" His voice grew gentle like he was approaching a sleeping bear. Ash selected a dirty dark green t-shirt and put his leather jacket over top of it.

"Alan." Ash took a breath. "Look, I don't really want to go talk to everyone." He laughed for the first time in a long time, "Plus, Sita would hate hearing them talk about her." That was my whole M-O when I was alive, but I wanted this for some reason that my ego could never reveal. "I get that," Alan replied disappointedly.

"Just between us, man," Ash said, picking up the phone to speak into it. "I'm going to go. But I'm not going to walk. I want to see the whole thing from afar. I'll be somewhere in the audience where fewer people are likely to recognize me, you know. But I'll be there."

"Honestly, I'm just happy to hear that, man. I'll be so much happier knowing your somewhere here. I have to go line up for rehearsal. If you want to meet up, I'd love to. Just know that I am here for you."

"I know you are," Ash said, hanging up.

Ash did know that Alan was there for him, but it didn't do anything to make him feel better. He didn't know that I was there for him too, and that didn't make him any better either.

He paused and looked at himself in the mirror. He took an extra moment and styled his thick golden hair. He looked at a picture of us in a photo booth taped to the mirror. My wild hair tried to take over the whole booth, and his big smile cut in between it and smushed up against my face. He grabbed the photo, kissed it, and put it in his pocket. I had all of Ash, but he thought he only had a single picture of me. It still meant something to me that he did that. He went downstairs and grabbed the invite from the fridge. He looked around the house, almost expecting Tony and Theresa to somehow jump up and ruin the day. When nothing happened, he went out to the car and headed to our graduation.

When we arrived, the parking lot was packed. It was car after car, filled with balloons and people in suits and ties. His plan to not stand out was looking less likely with each person in a fancy outfit that walked by. Ash sat in the car and just watched the families for a while. I sat and did the same. All this time being dead, Ash and I were on different levels. When he was mourning, I was trying to talk. When he was angry, I was scared. When he was lonely, I never felt alone. But, at that moment, watching the families walk by, I think we both felt the same.

We both looked out at what we would never have. We

looked out and imagined how our lives might have been different. I imagined a world where we both came from these happy families. A world where after graduation, our two families would gather to have dinner to celebrate, and maybe Ash would propose. I pictured another world with Ash and I attending our daughter's graduation. I would be holding the hand of our toddler, and him holding a big bouquet of roses. That just wasn't how we were raised. These happy families were not our past, and they weren't our future either. Ash turned the car off, and I looked at him gratefully, for the moment he didn't know we shared.

He got out of the car and started walking to graduation. He got some looks here and there. But he blended in as best as he could. The graduation was at a small stadium in the middle of Hill Valley. They called it a stadium, but it was little more than a small stage and a large fenced-in park. There were rows of cheap silver seats for the graduates and then randomly placed black chairs in the crowd for parents and families.

Ash found a space leaning on one of the white fences. He cozied into the fence as if he might break and run at any moment. He didn't stand there long before the graduation music began, and the graduates began to walk to their seats. I felt excited seeing them walk out, but I soon felt disappointed when I realized I wasn't really here for anyone. Ash also looked uninterested in the graduates walking out and making it to their seats. So far, this was more like a date; Ash and I both underwhelmed until we eventually would dip at any social gathering was a routine we had when I was alive too.

Ash probably regretted leaning up against the fence. The

ceremony was much longer and more boring than he could have imagined. But for some reason, he didn't leave, and he didn't even sit down. Something about the whole terrible experience was still mesmerizing.

They mentioned me. After the terrible speeches and before the students began to walk. Our principal, Mrs. Hallow, had dark braided hair that went down her back. I never spoke to her, not once. I wondered if Ash ever did either. I wondered what she thought when she heard the news that I died. How much pain can you feel for someone you didn't know at all?

"As we all know, we are missing a student here today." I thought about how they missed me when I was there too. "We know that Sita would have been excited to graduate today and move on to her dream of college." That was an easy guess. "Today, we walk for her, and we remember her as the kind and strong girl she was." That was not true at all. I looked at Ash, who was surprisingly wiping a small tear from his eye. I guessed that being remembered poorly was better than not being remembered at all.

I watched student after student walk up and receive their diploma. I thought about each one. I watched the ones that I hated a little less, and I was strangely happy for them. I wondered whether I could leave Ash's side and walk on that stage myself. But I looked at him, his tired eyes and felt I owed it to him not to experience that walk.

The ceremony ended, and Ms. Hallow had the students stand. This next part felt surreal, like when I very first died. Everything seemed slower and blurry. She began, "You have worked over 12 years for this moment, graduates. In a moment, you will move your tassel to the other side to symbol-ize, you have graduated." I looked to Ash for a moment like we did something together. All the hands in the crowd of graduates moved the tassel in a wave.

Then the graduates removed their hats and prepared to throw them in the air. The hats went flying into the air in every which direction. I tried to look at just one but would drown in the beauty of them all raining down. Just like that, the moment that signified the beginning for so many was just another ending for me.

6

Murder

A few days after graduation, Ash woke up to his phone buzzing again on the other side of the room, where he had thrown it the day before. It vibrated against the old wooden floor and pulled Ash from a nightmare-filled sleep. I knew it was likely his work again. Since he began working at the local movie theater when he was 15, he was always a dedicated worker.

When he first got the job, he felt freedom in it. He knew that every hour and day that he worked was an inch closer to true freedom. Once Ash and I started dating, he saw it as the only way he could provide for us. He would leave school early for work and wouldn't complete homework because he would stay there late. School felt so immature to him. He didn't understand how writing a literary analysis of *To Kill a Mocking-bird* was in any way beneficial to him. He understood it for the other teens, who didn't have real problems but were just creating them to pass the time.

Over time he had grown to dislike his job more and more.

He had to wear this worn-down green vest every day and stand almost all-day checking tickets. He didn't talk about it, but he didn't know what would come next. He had put all his energy into this job and now didn't see a path to move on to anything else.

While the phone continued to ring, I tried to think whether or not he told his job what happened. I couldn't tell if they fired him or not by now, for not showing up. But I doubted that they had a long line of people waiting to take that job anyway.

It rang again.

He turned and looked at my side of the bed again, looked at me, even though he couldn't see me. He sighed and wiped a stray tear from his eye that I didn't even see fall. I tried to have a moment with him to make him feel me. He sat up slightly and brushed his hand down what had been my pillow.

"I'm here, Ash."

Ash turned around and slowly sat up in bed. He pressed his hands deeply into his closed eyes and took a deep breath. When he rose from the bed, I expected him to go to the bathroom or go grab cereal. Instead, he walked towards the closet and opened it. He gazed at my clothes for a long time. He looked both determined and dead at the same time.

I walked up and tried to kiss him, but he didn't feel it, and neither did I. He picked jeans and a t-shirt from his side of the closet, and although I had never seen anyone that so desperately needed a shower, he put the clothes on over his filthy body. He was finally going to move, go to work, see Alan; I didn't care what he did as long as we could both leave the house.

The phone began buzzing again, and he watched the ground shake like an old massage chair. He looked at the phone, and then he looked back at the bed. He walked back and fell right back into the bed as if pulled by some other force. He slept for another three hours before he woke up again.

This time when he woke, he walked past the phone on the ground and into the kitchen, not knowing that the phone was holding the darkest of secrets. He poured himself some expired cereal and milk and just ate in silence. He would starve soon. He would miss rent soon if he didn't move on with his life. Look at me, a ghost giving life advice. I wondered how long he could live like this. The thought was beginning to suddenly dig at me. I hit the bowl he was eating from out of frustration. That's when it happened. The bowl moved. He jumped a bit and looked around.

"Sita?" he whispered into the air.

I tried to hit the bowl again, but it wouldn't move. Whatever this was, it was bullshit. He sighed, looking into the air. His face changed from hopeful to anger. "Well, if this isn't Sita, then just fuck off." With that, he finished eating and left the bowl on the table with the piled-up dishes. I spent the rest of that day and night trying to hit the bowl again over and over again, like in some sort of time loop. I was reluctantly freed from the loop the next morning when I heard Ash's phone ring upstairs once again. I only really even knew time was moving because of when that phone would ring.

I went back upstairs to check that Ash was alright. He was sitting on his bed in the same clothes he put on yesterday and was staring at the wall. Then the phone again. He took a deep breath and walked over to pick it up. His eyes looked at it and suddenly grew wider and more awake, as if the notifications had brought him back to life.

"Shit," he said as he looked through the 50 notifications on his phone. A good portion was his work, and the others were friends, but then he noticed a number he didn't know had called ten times. He put the phone on speaker and set it onto the bed next to him as he began listening to his voicemails.

"Hey man, it's Jorge. I am so sorry for your loss. Sita was a good girl. Anyway, she has a couple things still here at the house if you want to come to grab them." This was the guy I rented a room from before I basically moved in with Ash. I hated that there felt like there was no time for Ash to mourn. His world was here, crying in bed, but the rest of the world needed more from him than usual.

"Ash, it's Alan, man give me a call."

"Hi Ash, this is Detective Ronaldson. I've been trying to reach you for two days. We found some items of Sita's. We now believe this was a homicide. We could use your input. Please contact me as soon as possible."

Ash got out of the bed and stood up wide-eyed. He grabbed the phone off the bed and replayed the message.

Ash tightened his grip around the phone and dropped to the ground. This time he didn't cry; his eyes were saying something else. Every other time he fell to the ground, I comforted him, as best as someone who couldn't be heard, felt, or seen could. But this time, I collapsed too. It was, of course, a feeling I had, and his grandfather confirmed it. Yet, hearing it finally said and confirmed felt like the wet cement had settled. Why didn't I remember? Who took my life from me?

I tried to think of everyone I ever hated, but the list was too long. I hated so many, but I couldn't think of anyone who hated me. The thought of someone feeling so hateful towards me that they would kill me made my self-doubt creep in. It made me think of all the times I hated myself, all the things I did that disgusted me. I let myself feel self-hate and empathized with a killer.

Ash rose to his knees and looked around with a look of terror. But we were both too intrigued by the news of my murder to have the mental breakdown that was gnawing at our skin. I knew that sometimes when all you want is to move, you have to stay still, and whenever all you want to do is stay still, you have to move. So, Ash pulled at his hair a bit and rubbed his eyes, and began dialing a number on his phone.

"Yes, I need to speak to Detective Ronaldson immediately."

His voice sounded so hoarse, like he was the one who had died and not spoken for too long. "Detective, this is Ash. Sita's... Sita's..."

Boyfriend. Boyfriend Ash.

"Sita's."

"Yes, Ash, it has been rather hard to get ahold of you."

Ash didn't respond.

"When we found Sita's body in the river, we told you it was suicide or an accident. We sent searchers back two days ago to see if we could find evidence of either. Unfortunately, we found evidence of homicide instead. We found some of her belongings that we believe are suspicious."

There was a pause, and neither of them spoke. Ash pushed his fingers through his now dull and dirty golden hair.

"Ash, I need you to come to the station so we can discuss what we found."

"I'll be there in thirty. Can I have her belongings?" He said as he pulled my green plaid cardigan into his lap.

"Not until everything is processed, and even then, Ash, I hate to tell you, but sometimes they are never returned. I understand you were the closest person to her; I'll try to get something to you if you can help me too."

Thirty minutes seemed like a long time, and I wondered if he would just fall back into bed and those tempting flannel sheets. He sat there for about a minute after he hung up. He raided his room as I watched helplessly. He opened each drawer like it was the scene of the crime. He was looking through all my things with suspicion. He had the right idea. I would have done the same. If there was any indication that anyone had murdered me, it probably would have been there. But I didn't think he would find anything.

"OK, Sita, if you can hear me, I need you. I'm sorry. I'm sorry that I wasn't able to protect you. But I need you now. If you are here, send me a signal. I am begging you."

He paused in silence and just looked around the bedroom, both expectantly and desperately. He fell to his knees again, and I just knew his knees must be black and blue from collapsing. I sighed and tried again. I shouted and yelled and tried to throw things. I used all the energy I had to be as loud and noticeable as I could be. I kept trying even after he got up and looked to the ceiling, and said, "Bye, Sita, I love you." and walked out the door. I knew this was really goodbye for him. But I couldn't say goodbye and couldn't even feel the possibilities of it.

I heard the door open, and suddenly I was in Ash's car driving with him to the police station. He was dead silent. I couldn't shut up. I was having an imaginary conversation with him.

Come on, Sita, what was the last thing you remember? I imagined him asking.

"*It's really blurry, Ash, it's hard,*" I said, looking to him in desperation.

OK, then what's not hard? What's the last memory you have?

"*I was having breakfast at the Tree Diner down the road.*"

"*I am trying to remember what I ate.*"

That's not important, Sita.

"*OK, I was planning; I was planning your birthday.*"

His birthday. I completely forgot about his birthday. Not that I could have done anything for him, or that I even knew what day it was. But it must have come and passed. No one did anything. He was 19 now, and I was ... forever 18.

The police station was a small building blended in with other shops on the street, besides the little sign that said Hill Valley Police on the lawn. Ash parked his car and entered the station to find an older man with bright white hair at the front desk. The man seemed pretty uninterested. Ash walked up to him, and I realized at this point that Ash looked like a crazy person through and through.

He was consistent with his nervous habit of running his hands through his hair, which with the dirt and grease now, made it stand straight up like a mad scientist's. He was in his blue sweatpants and worn out grey t-shirt; both looked like they had lived through two more lives than they should have.

Ash told the older man his name and that he was here to

speak to Detective Ronaldson. The man at the desk looked him up and down skeptically before picking up the phone. When the man reached Detective Ronaldson, he seemed surprised to find that Ash actually had a meeting scheduled. "This way, son." He said with a slightly friendlier demeanor than before.

He took Ash into a small room with an old couch that looked like it had seen some things and two faded blue pillows. Across from the couch sat an even dirtier leather maroon chair. I wondered whether they were intentionally uncomfortable. The walls were bright white in a way that made me feel like it was meant to disorient me. I wondered how it was possible to have walls that white with furniture that dirty. Everything about it felt purposeful and vindictive.

Detective Ronaldson walked in with an attitude like he'd already solved the crime. He was a large man with a large mustache that should have had its' own name. He matched it with glasses that were far too big for his face, making his face a collage of 'stache and glasses. He sat in the maroon chair, and the chair groaned in pain against the weight. The green file folder he was holding was placed on his lap, and he had it with a firm grip. I think he smiled, but it was hard to tell. He pulled out a recorder from his grey jacket pocket and pushed play.

"Ash, nice to finally meet you."

His voice did not match his stern appearance. I imagined that must have been a constant battle for him. I imagined him trying to make his voice harder and sterner in his younger days as a detective.

"I will be recording this conversation, so I can review it

later. You may have clues you don't even know you have. First off, how are you feeling?" He said disingenuously.

Ash was obviously not here for pleasantries either and did not fall for the Detective's half-ass attempt.

"What do you have?" Ash responded coldly.

I sat down next to him as he spoke to the Detective as if I was being questioned as well. I placed my hand over his to provide myself comfort more than him.

"Well, we have her purse." He paused and looked at Ash for a response.

Ash stared back at him without flinching. Detective Ronaldson lowered his eyes a bit like a teacher trying to catch a student in a lie. But Ash lowered his eyes like a principal trying to catch a teacher in a lie.

Detective Ronaldson continued,

"Which is very helpful, but only to an extent. Now, we need your help. I know this is a difficult question, and you may not be able to answer it, but I need to know what the usual contents of her purse were."

We both took a moment in contemplation. Ash had done his share of digging through my purse. It was an old brown leather one with a dragonfly burned into the front. I bought it from a thrift store as a teen, and it never left my side since. He always used to throw his own keys in there when he didn't want to carry them. I thought of my regret realizing that my purse was probably half full of trash, which would make it difficult for the police to determine anything significant.

"Let me try this another way, boy."

I shivered at his use of the word "boy" because I knew the connotation would strike Ash as terribly insulting. I looked at him. I worried for a moment that if he lost his cool, the police would think he really was crazy.

"Her aunt told us she always carried pepper spray, is that correct?"

"Ya, she would have that. She would also have some makeup and her wallet. She was paranoid about crime. She wouldn't have let this happen. That's why this is so ridiculous. No one was more prepared to be attacked than her. Not that she had enemies, it was just she was always scared."

For a moment, I felt like he looked right at me because directly after he spoke, he slightly turned his eyes. The Detective wrote as Ash talked.

"I mean, that's what I know. But I don't know. She could have had stuff in there I didn't know about. Why?"

"No, that is very helpful, Ash. It's not about what else she could have had in there; we are more interested in confirming what should have been in there but wasn't. "

Ash was getting visibly upset with the Detective's hints without clues.

"You see, Ash, there wasn't any pepper spray or her keys. Her car was at the scene, but not her car keys. We find that suspicious."

"Did they fall out? You said you found her body in the river? Don't you think any of that could have fallen out of her pocket when she drowned? You think the murderer has this stuff? Like some sort of weird-ass trophy?"

"Slow down, young man." He closed the file and sat up a bit straighter in his chair.

"Her keys or pepper spray haven't been located. We find it suspicious that two key items from her purse that could be linked to safety are missing. We saved some clothes before she was cremated. It seems as though there was a small struggle. Can you tell me what her keys looked like?"

Ash flew into a rage. It was like a switch went off. I tried to calm him, shouting, *"Please, please, Ash!"* He started yelling at the Detective,

"Well, what the fuck are you doing here? Why aren't you out looking? Who did this to her? Tell me!"

Ash was now standing above the chair. The Detective waited a moment till Ash stopped yelling.

"Ash, I am looking. I'll ask you one more time. What did her keys look like?"

Ash took a deep breath and sat back down in the chair, aggressively running his hand through his hair. "I don't know. They had this like blueish puff on it."

Detective Ronaldson wrote that down. "Go home, Ash. I'll call you if we find anything or if I need to speak to you again."

Ash looked up with anger burning in his eyes. But he got up and left.

His mood was different the for the rest of the day. He wasn't mourning and living in his pain as much as he was before. He took a shower, a long and almost seductive shower. He then grabbed a large garbage bag and walked around the house, throwing away the weeks of trash and food that he left out. He sat down after that and got on to his computer. He searched my name, over and over, as if he were trying to find if I was living a secret life of some sort.

After a day of cleaning and searching and searching, he went to bed at 2 am, and I laid next to him like I did every night. After about two hours, he woke up and looked at where

I was lying, and, with wide eyes, he jumped from the bed. I got up too and saw the bed rise back up, from being dented down where I was lying.

I was excited. He was angry. "I won't keep saying this. Whatever is there, just leave me alone." He grabbed a blanket from the bed and went to finish sleeping on the couch. This time I stayed in our room and cried for the rest of the night.

Around 6 am, he walked back into the room, and I was still crying, sitting on the floor, with my back up against our bed. He walked right past me and went to the closet. He put on a clean pair of jeans and a red t-shirt with a local band logo on it that said, "Midnight Moon." When he went downstairs to have coffee, I stayed, crying. I didn't really have him. In fact, he thought I was just some ghost haunting him. I didn't have my life anymore because someone killed me. Now I don't even have an afterlife because I couldn't do anything other than follow Ash around and scare him.

Suddenly, I was in the car again—one of the many drawbacks of this afterlife. I had no say as to when I stayed or went from home. I wiped my tears and looked at Ash then back out the window as he drove through the red trees that were embracing Fall, and I recognized the drive. Ash was returning to work.

7

Jealousy

He pulled up to the movie theater and parked in a faraway spot. It was the local theater, mostly occupied by teens trying to get away from their parents. His growing bitterness towards the job had made him feel like walking into it was him sacrificing his happiness for his mother and me.

Despite his growing angst towards the job, Ash was still good at it. He was good at almost everything he did, whether he wanted to be or not. Someone could hand Ash an instrument at a party, and he would play like he had been playing his whole life. When we went to parties, this meant he got a lot of attention. At work, it meant he got a shift manager badge and could schedule his own ten-minute breaks. I wondered if he would ever go to college or if he would let my death ruin his life-our life.

The movie theater was large and outdated. When you first walked in, you'd see the ticket desk. It was a long-mirrored surface with a couple of despondent teens in windows selling tickets to films between texting their friends. If you walked to the right after the ticket desk, there was an old and untrustworthy elevator, with a torn-up orange paper that said, " For Employee Use Only" He took out his key and entered it into the slot to take the elevator down to the staff lounge in the basement.

I saw a young girl in the elevator as the door slowly opened. She sat in the corner with a puffy pink dress stretched over her legs and a messy blonde bun on her head. I noticed that Ash didn't see her as he stepped on. I felt hesitant about riding this sketchy elevator before there was some creepy little girl ghost in it, so now I felt even more uncomfortable as we entered. The metal door closed and then a metal cage door within as we entered. I looked at the little girl. She was staring towards the ground; her teary eyes began to clear instantly.

"Hi, I'm Sita."

She smiled.

"I'm Kyra."

Like my voice had lifted her from a coma, she jumped up into a standing position.

"Hey, what does that shirt mean?" She yelled excitedly.

I was forever wearing my torn-up jeans and a *Jurassic Park* t-shirt. It suddenly hit me that I could be facing an eternity of discussing *Jurassic Park* with other ghosts. Before I could explain, the elevator opens, and I followed Ash off, looking back at Kyra. She looked incredibly sad and returned to sit back down into the corner of the elevator, but this time waved at me as she sat and covered her knees with her dress again.

The encounter with Kyra impacted me in an odd way. It had me reflecting on my own existence. I felt like I had been numb to thinking or feeling emotions too much. When there was so much time to think, sometimes all you wanted was to do none of it. But seeing Kyra made me wonder if I was actually lucky. That poor girl seemed trapped in the elevator. I couldn't imagine that sort of existence. I felt fortunate for my agonizingly confusing world following Ash.

Ash walked into the break room. There were a couple of orange tables, an old fridge that wasn't aging well, and a large vending machine. Two teens were in there chatting and showing each other something on their phones. Ash seemed more confident as he walked past them, and he held his head high. I think he felt he had to be stronger than ever before, especially since everyone knew what happened to me. He walked to the backroom, a custodial closet that they had changed into an office for himself and the other shift leads.

He immediately opened some mail left on the desk. The room wasn't particularly large. It had room for the two turquoise chairs in front of his desk. Between the door and the chairs, there was only enough room for me to pace, though, and pace I did. I didn't just pace. I created energy of panic all around me. Ash radioed in to tell the crew he would be on the door. He threw his keys into the drawer, paused at the small mirror, ran his hands through his hair, and then walked out.

There was a new addition to the break room. A beautiful girl had arrived, and I instantly rolled my eyes. She didn't sit with the other two in the room. She had her whole body facing the door that Ash walked out of. She looked a few years older than us and had long chestnut hair with bright green eyes that I had to assume were contacts.

I never just dropped into Ash's work when we were together, or I mean when I was alive. I was never that type of girlfriend. But I was the type of girlfriend that used fake realities to put me at ease. I always told myself that everyone who worked with my boyfriend must have been ugly creatures of some sort, not bombshells like this girl. If I had known he worked with this girl, I would have undoubtedly stopped by more often.

"Ash, it's so good to see you."

His name melted out of her mouth. It was the voice of a literal fucking angel. The slight red tint sitting on Ash's face showed that he knew all this as well. "Emma, you too."

"Will you be here for a full day? Maybe we could get lunch." She said with the lure of a succubus.

"I probably won't be able to today."

He walked by the table and towards the elevator, and I walked behind him, feeling triumphant. But then he stopped, and I moved right through him as he turns around.

"I'll be open for it tomorrow, though."

She twisted around in her chair, revealing big beautiful white teeth and a skirt so short I could almost see up it.

"Great. I look forward to it." And with that, the real nightmare began.

I had another brief moment with Kyra. Even though seeing Ash want to date again was eating me alive, I decided not to take it out on her. Instead, I told her all about *Jurassic Park*. When we got upstairs, Ash went to a booth at the door between concessions and the theaters. He stood there for hours, taking people's tickets and directing them to the theaters.

There was a sinister foreign urge to make him feel what I

was feeling. Make him feel like the world was crashing down and not moving all at the same time. A hint of anger lingered for him. I couldn't believe this. I was attached to Ash forever because I loved him so much, and he was that quick to go on a date with another woman?

What was I supposed to do?

Would I spend my undead life as their third wheel?

Then I started picturing all the things I would have to be there for throughout his life. I couldn't be there for all the moments, all the memories that were mine. I would be there for new moments with new girls. I hated her, and for a moment, I felt that I hated him too.

The day finally ended, and I thought about as many terrible scenarios and things that could possibly exist. I figured nothing could possibly make this day any worse until he packed up to leave with a jauntiness and speed that made me suspicious. The second the clock hit 6 pm, he left his spot and scurried towards the front booth where they sold the tickets.

Sure enough, she was sitting in one of the booths, that evil Emma. Her head was down as she scrolled through Facebook. He whipped around the desk to the front of it.

She paused her Facebook scrolling and slowly looked to Ash, like out of a stupid hallmark movie.

"Ash, how was your first day back?"

There was that beautiful, awful voice again.

"It was good. It's weird to be back ."

Then he paused, and a solemn look completely overtook his face. It was as if he had just remembered why he hadn't been at work. At that moment, I was happy. I felt incredible joy that he had just remembered how incredibly dark the world was without me. She pulled him out of it with words that were laced with an even sweeter voice.

"It must be difficult, Ash; I hope you know I'm here for you. She is always with you too, but you have to move on. That's what she would want."

I burst towards her and even thought I saw her flinch. I yelled as I tried to hit her, move her, and see her flinch more, so I wouldn't think it was my imagination. "You don't know shit about me. You don't know me! I am stuck here, with him, maybe forever, or at least until he dies! And you think in your distorted little brain that I want him to move on!"

Ash nodded at her kind words and pulled me back into the elevator, although I could have stayed trying to hurt her for another eight hours, at least. As the door closed, and her manicured face was no longer visible, I took a deep breath. I looked to Ash and then the small ghost girl to my right. She actually scared me a bit. She was standing incredibly close and looking up to me like I was her long-lost mother.

"You came back!"

I stared out the doors with Ash, like we were both just normal humans getting off work.

"Well, ya, Kyra, that's how elevators usually work."

My kindness to the little girl had deteriorated with Ash's last conversation with Emma. Children have a way of grounding you, though, so it didn't take long for my demeanor and mood to shift.

"Do you come across a lot of people that don't come back in the elevator at some point?"

"I guess not, but most of them can't talk to me. I've got it the worst in here. There are almost no ghosts following around people that get into the elevator. We have a couple ghosts and mediums, but I can only briefly say hi before the elevator moves again. It's like I never get quality time with anyone!"

At that moment, the elevator doors opened, and Ash was already out.

"Sorry," I said without looking back at her.

I had my own problems; I just didn't have time for hers right now.

Ash tossed and turned all night, sometimes hitting right through me. When he woke up, he went to get ready again. This time he made some coffee and left it out on the counter. I missed it, that smell of freshly brewed coffee that travels through the entire house, and out of instinct, I tried to pick the coffee cup. I just wanted to feel that warmth. Unexpectedly the coffee cup fell when I reached out to it. The mug broke, and the coffee spilled out across the floor.

Ash came running down the stairs. When he saw the coffee, he looked drained, "What the fuck is happening?"

He threw a towel over it and went to leave for work. I sat in the car with him, angry at how he was moving on. I wanted to talk to him, to tell him how I felt, but I knew it was no use.

We got into the elevator, and Kyra was there again, sitting right in front of the elevator entrance.

"Hey! I was hoping you would come back again, so how'd you die, Sita?"

"I don't know," I responded, frustrated with the day already.

"Kyra, isn't there someone you love that you could go be with and watch over?"

"Not yet. I don't know that anyone loved me when I was alive either. So, I guess I'm just stuck here where I died until I find the person who killed me." She shrugged her shoulders.

"Is this where you died?"

"Yes."

Before I could learn more from Kyra, the elevator door opened again. I wished there was some way that Ash would stay in the elevator longer.

He exited, and soon, we were greeted by Emma, looking as beautiful as ever. This time she wore a black floral shirt that reached down to her cleavage, and I rolled my eyes. Even their ugly green vests for work didn't take away a thing from her beauty.

"Ash, so glad you're here again." She said while fluttering her big fake eyelashes, which were not there yesterday.

"It's nice to be back."

"We still on for lunch?"

"Sure," He said, acting like he didn't particularly care. I knew Ash better than anyone, even better than his invasive mother. I knew by the look in his eyes that he did, in fact, care.

8

Hope

After talking with Emma, Ash walked back towards the makeshift office and closed the door. He listened to overdue voicemails and wrote them all down. Then he pulled up to the computer. Usually, that meant he was preparing to make schedules or work on payroll.

Instead, he opened google and began typing. **I think my house is haunted.**

The first link he clicked on was a ghost story about an old cursed house that no one wanted to buy. I decided it was a good thing he was researching this because maybe he would realize that it was me the whole time.

How to know when you should get help for a violent ghost.

So, that was it; that was what he thought of me. He once loved me so much he couldn't contain it, but now I was just the violent ghost in his house. Are we all lying when we look into someone's eyes and say forever? Here I was offering him forever, and he couldn't see it. I wondered for the first time whether I was the one in the worse situation. The one-sided relationship was torture enough, but now he feared me.

This google search lead him to definitions of a dangerous ghost. The feeling of being watched, loud noises, walking, and breaking items. I thought about the coffee mug. All I wanted was to hold coffee, that simple pleasure one last time. Did I deserve to hold that cup of coffee? Because it seemed to me now that my desire for such a small pleasure had consequences I couldn't really understand. Ash cleared the search bar.

How to get rid of a ghost

I looked at Ash, and I saw anger in his eyes. He hated me, but he didn't even know it was me he hated. At this point, if I knew of a way, I would have left. I didn't want to scare him, and I wanted him to move on. When I was honest with myself, I knew I wanted him to fall in love again, but I didn't' want to be there to see it.

He found small hacks, put salt by the door, burn sage, light a candle, and ask it to leave. But he scrolled past all these ideas and found the services.

Ghost Hunter/Medium

Michelle May

A medium that will come into your house and rid it of any ghosts that are bothering you. Fast, easy, and reliable. Call now

He picked up his cell phone and called the number. I sat on the teal chair and just watched.

"Hi, I saw your ad online about getting rid of ghosts."

"Yes, I think my house is haunted, and the ghost seems to be becoming more violent."

"It's an old house, I'm worried something might have been there, or maybe something followed me there? Is that possible?"

"Yes, I feel exhausted. I recently experienced a loss. Maybe it triggered whatever is so angry in my house."

"Well, what would you do?"

"How much would that cost?"

"How soon can you come?"

"Sounds great, thank you." He said with a look of relief as he put the phone down. Then he began to pull up the scheduling document and actually started doing his job. What would this mean for me?

Then it hit me, and I felt relieved—a medium coming to the house. If mediums could actually speak to the dead, then maybe all my problems would be solved. She could tell him it was me; I could talk to him again. What if we could just live together, him knowing I was there and loving me as if he could see me? I pictured him having coffee and facing me and talking to me each morning. I pictured us having a normal relationship, or as normal as it could be between a ghost and a human.

I saw my life with Ash in many ways. Sometimes when I was feeling down, I would imagine us running off together and living off the grid. I would do the gardening, and he would build our home hidden in the woods. No technology, no people, just us. More recently, I pictured going off to college and returning after graduating to run away and elope in Vegas together. Then comes our own white picket fence.

Our vision wasn't a typical white picket fence. It would be more like a brown wood fence overgrown with vines. We would dance, garden, have children, and grow old together. But now these futures weren't for us. These ideal situations were so out of reach that the only realistic hope I had was that he would at least not be afraid of me.

Before I knew it, it was the dreaded lunch with Emma. He picked his brown coat up and draped it over himself. I followed him like a prisoner following their executioner. When we walked out and around the corner, we saw Emma already in the break room, staring at her phone once again. When he saw the back of her head sitting in that chair, he ran his fingers through his hair. This time I knew it was from his excited nerves.

She turned around in her chair when she heard him approach. She smiled at him and grabbed her light tan leather jacket that was far too small and frail to actually keep her warm. She also reached into the chair next to her and lifted a flawless Gucci bag. She got up and smiled, and I noticed her tidy makeup and hair up in a perfect ponytail.

I looked at Ash in disgust, then looked down at my grunge outfit and felt my messy long curly hair. How could he possibly go from being in love with me to liking her? Maybe he never loved me. Death and heartbreak have a way of showing just how bullshit love really is. All the times they say, "it is only you," and the "you're the only one" is revealed as the most desperate of lies.

She suggested they take the stairs. He took the stairs with her, and I followed, the whole time thinking to myself bitterly how I would never take the stairs if I were alive, wondering if he liked that about her more than me. I reluctantly followed them as they walked outside. Fall colors were blooming on the trees, and kids played at the park across the way.

They took a left towards a small pizza place that was right next to the theater. The pizza place, Emilio's, had a black and white sign that said seat yourself with a large smiley. Ash looked to Emma for direction, and she picked out a small table in the corner outside.

A large red umbrella hovered over the small table, and I suddenly felt like I had more in common with that umbrella than with Ash and Emma. Lunch was uncomfortable. They both ordered a slice of pizza and had an awkward first date conversation, which gave me true joy.

"I forget, were you born here in Hill Valley?" He asked.

"No, I moved here from San Diego. It was a big change, going from a bigger city to a small one like this." She twirled her hair and continued, "But, it's a nice change. I like it here. Makes me feel like I could really settle down. I love all the trees and how friendly the people are. It made me feel at home for the first time like this is where I was always supposed to be."

A silence followed, and I remembered that with Ash and I, our silences in conversation weren't strange, they were comfortable, but this was just the opposite. It was a silence of failure. Emma didn't let it last for long. "Look, Ash, I'm really sorry about your girlfriend." She looked genuine, and for some reason, I didn't like that even more than if she hadn't been.

He blew out some air and responded, "Thanks. It's been hard, but I feel like I'm finally feeling a bit better. I knew this would come up, to be honest. I want you to know that I feel ready."

She giggled, "Ready for what?" I gave him the look of death as if he could see me.

"Ya Ash, ready for what?"

"I just mean..."

She gave him a sympathetic smile, which made him change the subject quickly, "Anyway, what's your plan now? I know we both just graduated. Are you just going to stay at our dump job forever?"

That's all. That was what I was, a footnote in this awkward conversation. They continued like this for about 30 minutes. This surface-level conversation that doesn't actually teach you anything about anything.

After the longest time I felt of my afterlife, they left and decided to sit on a bench at the park across the street, with the 30 minutes remaining they had on their lunch break. The white bench faced a playground but wasn't too close. The kids were playing, and young women surrounded them like they were hired security. I wasn't listening much to what they spoke about. I couldn't bear it any longer. I was walking closer to the children. This was the first time Ash had really been outside, and I was testing how far away from him I could get. I tried to run, but I stayed in one place when I did that. So, I continued taking it step by step.

Suddenly, the women guarding their children perked up like lionesses who heard a branch break. I saw a man without a shirt and with jean shorts and a large smile, walking quickly up from the cattycorner to where Ash and Emma were sitting. The women all began calling their children over to return to them as he got closer and closer to the playground. A few children were left with leftover mothers trying to lure them out from the slide and under a bridge. They were desperate and only breathed when they saw the man stop before the playground. He stopped instead, right in front of me. He looked at me square in my dead eyes.

I turned to see Ash and Emma deep in a conversation. I noticed that their knees were slightly touching. But they didn't see what happened, which is why I had initially looked over anyway. I wanted them to notice that I was finally being noticed. The man wore an old spiked choker around his neck. When we opened his mouth, I smelled cigarettes and years of not brushing.

"Well, hello."

I looked behind me to see if I was mistaken and he was speaking to someone near me instead.

Then I turned back to look at the man. "Are you dead?" I asked, even though I knew deep down that he wasn't.

"No, I'm a medium. Dave's the name. I talk to living, I talk to dead, and who my dear are you?"

"This is great. Please, sir, I need your help." I pointed towards Ash. "It's my boyfriend. He doesn't know it's me following him. But I need him. I can only move if he moves. So, he has to know, he has to be with me too, and right now he is only scared of me."

Dave adjusted his choker a bit and looked back at Ash.

"You know the living run from the look of me." He said, pointing to the mothers who were all holding their children tight. "But the dead aren't much better. They always want something from me." He said, giving me an annoyed look.

"Why do you want him to notice you so bad anyway? If you want to be noticed, you should really start haunting your murderer instead."

Ash finally looked up at the man. He continued to listen to whatever bullshit Emma was spilling, but now also kept an eye on Dave at the same time.

Ash's expression had grown concerned as the man staring him down talked so passionately to the air.

"Why would I attach to my killer stronger than Ash?"

"Sweetie. Our souls are all about attachment. Just like our souls when they are living, we attach to the bad so much stronger than we ever attach to the good."

"If they find my killer, and I'm stuck with them forever, can I ever see Ash?"

"No, probably not, unless he also becomes a ghost. Even then, it would be almost impossible to find each other. But if you're scaring him, maybe you should just move on."

"Ok, well, this isn't even an option right now. I have no real clues about who did this to me. There's a chance I'll never know." I pictured never seeing Ash again. "I think maybe I'm ok with that. But if we can get Ash to know I am here, maybe he won't feel tortured. Can you help me, Dave?"

Dave gave me a sweet smile for the first time, "I can try."

Dave began to walk towards Ash and Emma on the pearl bench.

"Excuse me, sir," Dave said, almost aggressively.

Ash grabbed Emma's arm and stood up.

"I don't have anything," Ash responded as he pulled Emma away.

"No, I don't need anything. I need to talk to..."

But before he could finish his sentence, Ash was quickly ushering Emma away and back to the movie theater. As he rushed away, I had no choice but to join. I reached towards Dave as I was pulled back towards the movie theater.

9

Pain

The next day was the weekend. Thank God. I couldn't bear to look at Emma again. I wanted so badly for Ash to get out and live his life again. Now, all I wanted was the opposite. All I wanted was for the broody and dirty Ash to return. He was awful. But he was mine and only mine.

I watched him sleep. This time I sat on the small windowsill instead of lying next to him. It was a moment of peace for me again—a moment with just us. So much happened in the past few days. Between wondering if I would be doomed forever and watching the man I love fall for someone else, I was losing myself.

I remembered, looking at his sweet face, who I was before all of this. I was beautiful and spunky. I had an attitude that only Ash understood. I loved to write music and garden. I would cook Ash pasta, almost every night, a different recipe because I would get too bored too quickly. But I knew pasta was his very favorite.

I wasn't that person anymore, though. I couldn't do any of

those things. I couldn't love. I couldn't fight. I couldn't really exist. I was beginning to feel empty, to feel like a shell of what was. But sitting here looking at the man I loved so much, I felt something again. I felt like a human for just that moment. I jumped as a loud knocking started on the front door.

I knew the medium was supposed to be coming today to help him with that terrible violent ghost. Suddenly, I was scared, what if the medium could get rid of me? What would happen to me? As he rustled in the bed, I jumped up, knocking over the plant that sat on the window. It came crashing to the ground, and Ash bolted up. He looked at the mess and sighed with frustration, but before he could take it in too deep, the knocking continued.

I said sorry into the air as if it made a difference.

He grabbed his ratty brown robe off the door that he hung it on and headed to the front door. To my relief, when he opened it, it was his mother again with a casserole in her hands and a bright teal dress that felt blinding.

"Oh, good, you're up." She said as she pushed by him and into the kitchen. Her ghostly grandfather trailed behind and offered me a genuine smile as he entered. A few steps behind was Tony, holding an egg casserole that he was about to spill.

Ash grabbed the egg casserole from Tony's drunk hands and followed his mother. I reached out for him like I had the first time she visited, but this time nothing happened. He sat at one of the bar seats. His mother unwrapped an egg casserole and put it into the oven to hear, while Tony sat next to Ash and put his head down on the table.

"You look much better, Ash, finally coming to terms with what happened?"

"I don't think it's something I'll ever quite come to terms with, Mom, but sure, I've begun to live my life again. Without her."

I felt uneasy as I felt his great grandfather look at me with pity.

"Well, good. You know, Ash," She moved towards him and put her pale hand on his dark face. "You are so good looking and so smart. You have a beautiful life ahead of you."

She slowly pulled back and went over to the oven to check on the casserole, even though she had just put it in. She seemed almost sober. Still incredibly rude and uncaring, but possibly sober.

"Sita was always so different too. You never know; she could have been holding you back. Always this talk about art and travel, the most unreliable way to live."

Ash looked at his mother's back towards him as she faced the oven, and anger suddenly flooded his eyes.

"You didn't know her." He said with a strained voice that made me cringe. This almost woke up Tony, and with his head still on the table, he mumbled. "Don't you talk your mama like th."

"I'm not sure anyone did. She was so rude. I just feel like you could do better, that's all."

Ash's eyes burned a hole through her, and he remained silent. I looked to her grandfather, who sat back on the floor and began tracing the tiles with his fingertips.

She continued after the uncomfortable pause, which was uncomfortable for more people than she knew.

"Now no more talk of that anyway, Ash. Have you returned to work?"

Ash was clearly over his mother, sober or not, and didn't answer. She pulled the casserole out of the oven, still cold.

"Do you know anything more about her death?"

"I know someone murdered her; I know I'm going to find out who it was."

His mother turned even paler. She dug into her purse and put on her too square glasses. One thing I noticed about her was that she put these glasses on whenever she was doing something important.

"What do you mean murder?

"Well, they brought me in for questioning, and I don't know. But cops don't do anything. They don't solve anything. They believe that she was murdered." He ran his hands through his hair. "Her body was found in the river. That's all they will tell me. So, I'm going to do whatever it takes to solve it myself. "

She looked more worried than she had been this whole time. Ash looked at the time on his phone.

"Look, Ma, I've got some plans today. "

"What plans?"

She must have wondered why Ash never seemed to really want to spend time with her when she actually was around, but to me, it wasn't a mystery at all.

"Just plans, Ma. I am a grown-ass adult, and it's really none of your business."

He didn't typically talk to her like that, but this whole meeting had felt tense and out of place. He usually spoke to her more like a child, and he was afraid of breaking her. It was a delicate balance he had to have between keeping her alive while not supporting her lifestyle.

"Well, fine." She said spitefully, putting her glasses back into her navy floral purse and fluffed her hair a bit, looking at him angrily.

"We need to speak more about this, though, Ash. Come on, Tony." She said, hitting him on the head to wake him up, but he didn't move at all. I wondered if Tony was dead for a moment, and I would be stuck for eternity in this home with him, at which point I would most definitely become evil. I kept my eye on Tony as they spoke and was incredibly relieved when he grunted and moved his head to the side.

"Sure," Ash said, not looking up from his breakfast.

She made a huff like a small child and walked out of the kitchen. Then yelled back, "Tony! We are leaving." Ash gave Tony a push, and he fell from his chair. He shook his head and looked around. He leaned side to side as he got up and followed Theresa out the door. I followed them both out with my anger, hoping she would feel the bitter energy.

I went back to the kitchen and found Ash just moving the food around with his fork now. Seemingly deep in thought and unsure of what came next with the medium coming today. He got ready for the day. I perched at the window, looking for the medium. Dave, the medium at the park, told me how vital it was to get through to Ash.

I watched as an old silver Nissan pulled up slowly in front of the house. The door opened, and a young-looking woman with deep black hair and camo pants with a jean jacket came out of the car. She had jewelry hanging off every part of the body that it could possibly hang off. In her right arm, she had a large black beach bag full of items. I hit against the window, wondering if she could see me already, but she didn't even look up. I hit it again and again with desperation seeping from my dead bones.

She came to the door and rang the doorbell. I was yelling through the door, so excited that someone may be able to hear me. "*Hello! I'm here! Please help me! Help me!*"

I pressed my entire body to the door, trying to feel a connection to her. Ash opened the door, and it went right through me, and I was face to face with her. She wasn't looking at me. She was looking at Ash.

"Hello, I am Michelle. I am the medium here to cleanse your home. "

"Morning," he said with a half-smile, "Come on in."

He pointed to the living room, which had a black worn-in leather couch and two tan chairs to the side, with flowered Boho curtains hanging high above it all. She sat on our couch, and Ash sat in one of the tan chairs facing her. I sat right next to her.

"*Can you see me?*" I asked as I went to touch her arm.

She didn't respond, didn't flinch, didn't even seem to feel me.

I comforted myself by grounding in what I already knew about mediums. I assumed that she just couldn't talk to me straight out. That was Dave's strategy, and that made him look completely crazy. No one listened to him. Maybe she was smarter and purposely not talking to me just yet.

"So, tell me," she said with a raspy voice, "How can I really help you today?"

Ash stroked the slight stubble that was slowly beginning to appear. It made him look older and sexier. But I wondered if he would play with it nervously like he did his hair.

"I think I have a ghost and not a good one."

"Are ghosts ever good?" She said as she wrote things in her small black notebook.

"Well, I don't know. You see, I lost my girlfriend." He paused, "Ex-girlfriend, I guess."

I stopped staring at Michelle and quickly turned to look at him angrily. It just wasn't fair that he could move on. This was the first time I really felt gone for him. I thought that he was really going to move on if I didn't get to him.

"Anyway, I had hope for a while that maybe if an afterlife existed, she would reach out to me, but she never did."

"You think she could be the ghost?"

"I hoped, at first. But the timing was off first of all. After she died, I never felt her. I had already started to move on when I started noticing scary things around the house, which wouldn't be Sita. Whatever is here, just I don't know. It doesn't feel like Sita."

I turned back towards her,

"It's me. I'm his girlfriend. I'm here."

She began to speak again, and for a moment, I thought it was going to be in response to me.

"Well, Ash, I can tell you there is an afterlife. I can also tell you what is in this house." She paused and looked everywhere but at me. "It's not your girlfriend."

He started to put his hands through his hair and stopped mid-way as she spoke.

"If your girlfriend wants to reach you, she can reach me from the afterlife to tell you something. We can do that be-fore our cleansing if you would like. Of course, I would have to charge for that. I wish I didn't have to, but it's how I make a living. She can tell you some really important things, though, and I can feel her already. But I will tell you I can only speak to her on the other side. I can't bring her here. Once a spirit has moved on, they can't return."

"But I haven't moved on. I'm right here."

She continued, "But, I know you didn't call me here to contact someone on the other side. You called me because you were scared of what's in your house."

He sat up straight,

"I'm not scared. But something is here." He looked around the home.

"Like I said, at first I thought it could be my girlfriend. But it's not. It's bad energy. It's breaking things and hitting things." He looked around again for a moment.

"I think I feel it watching me sleep."

She wrote like some sort of therapist.

"Well, we can get it out of the home, don't you worry. We can also see if I can make contact with your ex. Let's begin there. That will surely be a comforting way to begin."

She took a black elastic band off her wrist and pulled her long dark hair into a tight ponytail, which made her baked-on makeup look even worse.

"As you must be able to understand, I need to get into the right zone to reach her. Do you have some hot tea you could make me?"

He took a deep breath and again reached for his incoming beard.

"Sure."

He got up, and as soon as he left the room, she jumped up. She ran over to our bookcase and quickly scanned over the books in it. Next, she moved over towards our dark brown entryway and opened the two small drawers, and began to rifle through our papers. I saw her read over a couple of pieces of mail and then pull out a greeting card. I gave Ash the card for his birthday last year.

She read it over, and then we both heard the whistle of a tea kettle from the other room. She tossed it back into the drawer and scurried back to the couch. She opened her notebook, wrote a few notes quickly, then put it down again, and began to pick at her nail polish. A moment later, Ash entered the room with a red striped mug steaming with tea and handed it to her. She looked up, surprised like she had been waiting the whole time.

"Oh, thank you." She took a small sip of the tea, and Ash went back to sitting in the tan chair, utterly unaware of her bizarre behavior.

He just stared at her, and suddenly she put the tea down and got a look over her face like she had seen something beautiful. She put a hand out towards Ash.

10

Who

"Someone, someone wants to speak to you, from the other side."

Ash leaned forward, intently in his chair.

"She is having a hard time coming through. She says something is blocking her, some evil spirit in the home."

I sat up and looked into her eyes,

"I didn't say that."

Ash went to speak, but she straightened her hand more to stop him.

"The name, the name, it starts with an S." Tears began to fill Ash's eyes.

"She is so young and beautiful. Is it Sita? Wait...maybe...maybe your honey."

"That's right," I said, *"Please tell him I am here, that it's me living in the house. I have no control over what I do. I don't mean to scare him."*

Ash wiped at a tear, " How'd you know that?"

"She's here. She has a message for you. She says she loves you; she misses you; she is in a better place."

What the fuck? I didn't say any of that.

I sat back in my chair, discouraged, then remembered the birthday card she had read.

"You could have read my name off the card. Are you even real? Can you see me? Hear me?!"

"She says that she knows you won't celebrate your birthday down here because you hate it. But wants you to know she is celebrating it every year in the better place for you."

Ash collapsed his head into his hands, unable to handle what he thought was clear proof she was speaking to me, and at the same time, I rose from the couch out of anger.

"Oh, you have to be kidding me. You're a fake, aren't you?"

I walked over to the bookcase she had looked through before and began trying to take out books to stop this charade, to send Ash a message, to be noticed. A book fell. Michelle opened her eyes and looked, and Ash did too, as it fell to the ground. Michelle looked more scared and surprised than Ash did.

"Sita says there is something bad here, something she wants to protect you from."

Ash faced back towards Michelle.

"Tell her I love her; tell her she will always be my first love." My anger was building.

"What about your last love?"

I yelled at him right near his face. All I had wanted for him to do was to talk to me. Now just didn't feel the same, though. I couldn't talk to him at all, and that was always the bigger problem.

"She says she doesn't have much time left." She said with a small smirk, seemingly proud of her vicious con. "She has to move on. She will be waiting for you on the other side when it's your time. But she wants you to live, to laugh, to fall in love again."

"Ask her who."

She put her hand up again.

"Ask again. She couldn't hear you; she is fading away."

"Ask her if she knows who killed her." He said, not looking up at Michelle.

Michelle opened her eyes, seemingly overwhelmed. She took a deep breath and closed her eyes again.

"She says. She says, a stranger."

I spoke as a pouted on the couch,

"I don't know if it was a stranger. I don't know who it was. I'm trying to figure it out, but it's complicated solving a murder when no one will talk to me or look at me."

"She says that you may never know. But just to know that she is at peace. She wants you to be at peace too. The stranger will get what is coming to him. He won't continue what he did to her."

"Is there anything I can do?"

"She is leaving Ash; she can't answer anymore. "

"Can she hear me still?"

"For just one more moment."

"I love you." He said into space as I sat right in front of him.

Ash quickly wiped the tears from his face.

"Now, let's get to the regular business." She said matter of factly as she pulled back open her small notebook and flipped to a new page.

"Let's get rid of the spirit haunting you in this home."

She began writing a small checklist. "We will be doing multiple different rituals to rid the house of the ghost. "

I knew I was farther away from him than I was before Michelle had come. I knew he needed to know I was here. He couldn't die naturally and assume I'd be on the other side because then he would move on, and where would that leave me?

Michelle pulled a pile of sage from her bag. "First, we will begin the cleansing with some sage. I will burn it, and as you walk around, I need you to be authoritative. You need to tell the spirit that they aren't welcome and to move on."

They both stood, and he followed her to the front door, which I could still see from my seat. She lit the sage, and I watched the smoke float across the room. I sat there, unimpressed and thinking as she began reading from her notebook.

"This house is cleansed leave spirit."

I rolled my eyes. But then I watched as they moved closer to me and the smoke came towards me. Suddenly, I felt a burning, as if knives were stabbing me over and over. I jumped up and away from the smoke.

"*Stop! Stop! That hurts!*" I shouted.

I moved back towards the door, thinking I could hide, but the smoke lingering there filled me with pain, so I ran past them and into the kitchen. The smoke followed and burned through me. I fell to the ground.

"Now say it with more authority Ash. Yell at the ghost to leave."

I huddled in the corner with my knees up and shaking with pain.

Ash's voice boomed.

"Get out of this house spirit!" and with those words, a new jolt of pain shot up my back, feeling like I was kicked.

"*Ow!*" I screamed as I fell forward into a fetal position.

They turned to leave and headed up the stairs that were directly in front of our front door. I wiped tears from my eyes and tried to see through the smoke. I had to escape, had to get away from the pain. But then I heard his voice call out from upstairs,

"Get out, this is my home!" and with that, the pain shot at my head, and I pulled at my hair.

"*Please, Ash. Please stop.*"

I got to my feet and shakily moved back into the living room. I curled up on the couch, waiting for the pain to cease. I had nowhere to go, I knew they were upstairs, and the closer I was to them, the worse the problem was. But the smoke lingered downstairs and burned at every piece of me. When they returned back down the stairs, Ash looked unphased, and Michelle had a smile on her face.

I felt the burning begin to release as they put the sage out, and the smoke started to lift. I sat up as they both came to sit back down. I looked at her heavy makeup and deep brown eyes. This woman was no medium and had probably looked up ways to get rid of a ghost online. She had no idea that what she was doing was actually torture for me.

"I believe, Ash, you have an older spirit here, male and angry. I think it could be attached to something or someone you brought into the house. So do keep that in mind, and maybe clear out your home of some physical clutter."

I couldn't believe how much bullshit could actually fit into this small woman.

"I think we can leave it at this. The ghost should have received the message. I will be checking in again in a week or so to see if you need me to come back and try a more aggressive approach."

I perked up at this, looking at her with a please in my face. I couldn't imagine what could be more painful or aggressive than what they had just done.

"Payment, I require 300 dollars in cash or check."

She smiled, and I knew she was proud of herself for conning him.

"Yes, of course." He said as he got up and into the drawers that she rifled through earlier to find out about me. He pulled a checkbook out of it and wrote the con artist a check for lying about me and torturing me.

The rest of the night, I didn't move from the couch. I cried and held myself in pain, and hopelessness flowed over me.

There was no way out, and just like when I was alive, things were only getting worse.

11

Love

I was beginning to question my relationship with Ash. How much pain can someone put you through before you walk away from them? Sometimes it feels infinite, which is why it's so hard to walk away. Of course, as much as I wanted to reflect on this, I wasn't even physically capable of leaving.

When I was about ten years old, my parents took me to the county fair. I remember being amazed by all the colors and sounds surrounding me. They held hands and walked in front of me, kissing every few minutes. Everything just felt incredibly magical, and if I knew how few moments like this, there would be, I wouldn't have ever left.

This was what I always saw from my parents, love like they just met. It made me think that that's just what love was. I was confused at school by stories of bad love, and I was even more confused that people sometimes didn't treat each other well. On the other hand, I was also confused when other kids at school told me memories that actually involved playing with their parents.

My memories, like this of the carnival, my parents were just in the background of the memories. It was like every experience I had was actually on my own. My parents believed that as long as they brought me to tag along to the carnival or the zoo, they were doing enough as parents; usually, it was. I never knew any different, but I imagined had I been blessed enough to not die before having my own children, that Ash and I would have done things very differently.

My parents and I loaded onto a small Ferris wheel. My parents sat on one side. My dad had his arm around her shoulder, and she was playing with his beard. They were whispering back and forth, and I turned to lean over and look at the view from my side. I watched all the people running around the carnival-like ants, and I spotted a clown running around chasing children. I turned around, "Mom! Dad! I see a clown chasing kids."

"Silly," My mom said, looking at me briefly. "Sita, you should stay more in the cart. You could fall out, and then what?" I turned around and sat back down with a terrible view of the carnival, thanks to my height.

When we got off the Ferris Wheel, my dad bought us both some Dippin Dots, and we sat on a grassy area to have some snacks. I was taking in as much as I could. But my dad was laughing and giving my mother small spoonfuls of Dippin dots. Another couple, a bit younger than my parents, came and also sat on the grass area. But something felt wrong right away. The guy had almost white blonde hair and large muscles that made me think he was cute for an older man. The lady was even prettier, with straight red hair that looked soft as silk. They were whispering aggressively initially, and I didn't know whether they were aware that I could still hear them.

He leaned in. "Listen, Daisy. We can fuckin leave right now if you're going to act like this."

She shook a bit as she spoke. "You are cheating again. I know it."

"Ok, we will fuckin leave if you're going to be this ridiculous."

"How about you leave, and I find someone to cheat on you with?" She said louder this time, and she gave him a small shove before she got up. He had a fire in his eyes as he stood with her. He grabbed her tightly by the wrist and pulled her away.

I remembered being so confused. The only real love I witnessed was between my Mom and Dad. I looked back at them. My mother was just smiling at me, and my father was smiling at her. They were oblivious to what happened because everything between them always seemed so sweet. Sometimes I could barely even get their attention because they were so in love. So, witnessing the other couple made me very uneasy. I couldn't imagine why people would be so mean to each other. I didn't understand why anyone would stay with someone when they hurt them. I didn't understand love yet.

I always imagined that Ash and I would end up like my parents, only hopefully live longer. But I pictured that we would never hurt each other. Those were promises we had made to each other before we hurt each other. I specifically remember that promise so vividly because we made them on the best night of my life. Nothing amazing had happened, but when you're that deep in love, the smallest things can feel like heaven.

It was Valentine's day, and I spent the day getting completely ready. I painted my nails and put temporary purple streaks through my hair while Ash worked for most of the day. He told me he had a special date planned for when he finished work. When his bright blue Jeep pulled up, I pulled on a little black dress, then jumped on the bed and pulled out my phone to try to look casual. But I didn't see him coming around the corner into the room. I saw perfectly bright roses in the doorway, then he pulled around and peered in with a sexy smile that made me forget the confidence I had just gained from getting ready. I put my phone down, and he handed me the roses, leaned in so close I fell back to laying down and kissed me.

"You look beautiful, honey. I'll be ready in about 30 minutes." He said, tucking a piece of my hair behind my ear. He took me to the fanciest restaurant I had ever been to. It was kind of dark but decorated with beautiful greenery everywhere.

We sat down at a small table with roses and a candle in the middle. A man in a suit walked up to us, handed us the menus, and even put the napkins onto our laps. Ash was dressed up in a white button-up that made him look like an adult. I looked into those deep brown eyes and literally felt like I was in a fairy tale. Our conversations were different than his conversations with Emma. They were as deep and as never-ending as the stars.

"Do you think your parents are in heaven?" He said, spreading butter across a piece of bread.

He was the only person who could ask me this sort of question without upsetting me.

"I don't know. Sometimes I feel like they are around me. But sometimes I think that could be naïve. Do you believe they are?"

"I don't know. I think that anything is possible. I also feel like you can believe whatever you want to believe. No one should tell us what we can and can't believe."

The server arrived with our meals, and I was surprised by how small and delicate they both looked.

I began talking once he walked away and while Ash took his first bite. "I'm happy they at least left me with some money. I think I want to use it to go to college."

"That's amazing." He said, pointing at the food. "As for college, where are you thinking?"

"I don't know, I've looked at here, but like we could just do long distance for a short time if I picked somewhere else too."

"Try your food, honey. It's so good." He pressed me, then responded. "My mom told me the other day that one day you're going to leave me."

I laughed, "Babe, you know it's not the same." I grabbed his hand, "I will always be with you."

He looked deep in my eyes and touched a bit of stubble on his face, "I know you won't."

"I sometimes worry that I'm too much like my mother, though," I said in between bites of the best gnocchi I have ever had.

"What do you mean?"

I stopped and said, "I don't know that I could ever live without you, like if something awful ever happened."

"Aw honey, it's not good to think like that. But you're a stronger person than your mother was." He put his hands through his hair and looked back at me. "We're stronger than our parents. Just like I won't be an alcoholic like my mom, or not even around like my dad, you won't be like your mother."

It was a strange thing to hear because I wanted to only be like my mother before she died. But now it was the one thing I really feared. When she was around, I thought she was perfect. The older I got, I saw that she wasn't so perfect. Her obsession with my dad didn't always lead to her being a good mom and eventually made her no mom.

We finished eating, and Ash gave me a kiss on the hand before we headed back to his place. When we got there, we saw Tony out front, lying out on the lawn like a star. We got out of the car. I leaned down.

"Tony?" First, seeing if he was dead. He opened his eyes about halfway, so I continued.

"What are you doing?" Ash stood off to the side, uninterested but watching me protectively.

"Damn, woman locked me out of the house."

"Maybe you should go home then, Tony."

"Naw, she will never let me back in if I do that." He sat up a bit and looked at me with a hand up as if the sun were in his eyes, but the sun was mostly down.

"Hey, you guys have a couple bucks?"

Ash intervened now, "Sure, Tony, I've got a couple bucks if you take it and leave."

Tony grabbed the money and walked straight down the street, with no seeable destination. We walked into the house and found that Theresa wasn't even home. Nothing made sense with those two. We laid in bed that night, and I was lightly tickling his arm wrapped around me. We were cuddled into each other like we'd become one person.

"Honey." He said into my ear. "We don't need our parents. One day everything will be better. It will finally just be you and I."

"I know, babe. Too many adults are hurting, and too many adults are hurting each other." I said.

He pulled me in tighter, and I felt so safe. "I'll never hurt you, I promise." I turned around and faced him, "I promise I'll never hurt you either." I said as I leaned in and kissed him. I wanted to keep that night forever. I took a moment and breathed in everything about it.

Now I was sitting on our couch in constant pain. Michelle left maybe an hour or so ago, but everything was lingering in the air. I counted the small bubbles on our ceiling, trying to tell myself that each one meant I was closer to not being in pain anymore. The middle of the night brought some relief.

Bubble number 8,203 I realized that the pain was low enough that I could move again. I moved to sit on the floor. I stretched my legs out. I looked through my legs and wondered how I could feel such pain from a body that was barely there. I pulled my hair out of my face and put my own arms around myself. Something always felt different since that day; the pain never completely went away.

I eventually went upstairs and found Ash sleeping soundly. He wasn't rolling around like he usually did. It seemed that my torture brought him some sort of relief. It was the first time he slept all through the night. It made me realize how much I was affecting him. Other than the strange presence at the funeral home, I also didn't think I had protected him from anything at all. All these distorted love stories we had seen, and somehow ours had become the worst.

12

Drugs

I didn't know how long it had been, maybe a few weeks. I was doing everything I could to keep my distance from Ash. The only problem was that the distance was never far enough. I knew if I scared him, he would have some other idiot come to our home and torture me. I tried to sit in the corner of the room, not touching anything for as long as possible.

Sometimes I couldn't sit there any longer. I would start twitching and fidgeting like I was losing my mind. Like I was becoming something I didn't recognize, becoming less human every day.

I couldn't bear those walls anymore. I had to walk around, look outside, anything. During these times of weakness, I accidentally switched the lights on, made a noise after accidentally running into the dresser, and on a really bad day, I shattered his mirror. I watched him pick it up, piece by piece, and some part of me was hoping he would cut himself. I resolved that day to never wish harm again, no matter what was screaming inside me to.

Things weren't any better for me at Ash's work. He rode the elevator, and I talked to Kyra every day. She told me stories about her childhood and life before she died. She tried to get stories out of me about being a teenager because she would never have those memories. But I always had to explain to her that my teenage years were mostly in solitude, then it was all about Ash, and now it wasn't even leading up to anything. I always hoped that I would really grow and live as an adult; being a teenager just wasn't for me. But I didn't know then that being a teenager was all I would ever have.

I would then be pulled along to Emma and Ash's now daily date at lunch. If you have ever watched the person you love fall in love with love someone else, you know it feels like being suffocated by sand. Now picture having to be there, having to watch every small moment of it. Maybe you would feel yourself drifting into the wrong place too. How strong am I? How long will I keep fighting darkness?

I wanted more than anything to stop having to ask myself these questions. When we would go to lunch, I looked for Dave and looked for hope, but I never found him or it. This wasn't a good life for me, or for Ash thinking that he was haunted continuously and living in fear. Last night I watched him toss and turn all night. I tried to gently touch him, calm him. Instead, he woke up, touched his cheek, and shivered. He stayed up all night after that. He sweated in bed and looked through his phone. Every couple of minutes, he would look around the room paranoid. I stayed still, sitting in the corner, hoping he would be able to rest. In the morning, we headed to his job despite his sleepless night.

When we got to the elevator, Kyra was waiting excitedly to see me.

"Morning, Sita!"

She seemed more excited than usual, and it made me kind of nervous. Something about Kyra was just never right. It was something I couldn't put into words, and if I could, I would keep those words hidden anyway.

"Morning, Kyra. What should our minute be about today?"

She just smiled and looked forward, which was not Kyra's style at all. She usually wouldn't stop talking for that precious minute. I looked her up and down. When she looked up at me, I was reminded of how young she really was, the innocence in her eyes, and I felt protective. But those big eyes and messy bun were holding something sinister in them.

The elevator jolted to a stop.

She shrugged, "Guess we have a bit more time today." She said with a smile that didn't hide anything.

Ash cursed in the corner and pushed at the buttons. I felt human fear and, for a moment, worried I would be trapped forever. But, remembered quickly that inconveniences like this aren't very important when you are already dead.

"Kyra," I said with a more mothering tone than I even knew I had. "How did you do this?"

"Wasn't me, I swear!"

I sighed. I didn't know what she did or how she did it. But how could I possibly blame her? I was miserable following Ash around day and night. I couldn't imagine being trapped in an elevator for eternity. I decided to take advantage of the situation instead of question what she did to make it happen.

I trusted her, even though as we spoke, she stared up at Ash like he had a dark target on his back as he cursed to himself.

"So, Kyra, if someone looked into your murder. If they found your murderer, you could move on to follow them, right?"

"Well, my murderer would be like a hundred years old. Even if they were still alive, I wouldn't be following them for long." There was a pause, and she looked at me like I was stupid, "Because then they would be dead."

I looked at Ash, trying everything to get his phone to dial out, but it appeared he didn't have service. I sat down, knowing we might be here for a while. Kyra came and sat right next to me. I looked at Ash as he pulled at his hair and looked around the elevator as if there would be a secret door he could escape from.

"I want to be with Ash. But, not like this. I want him to be with me, just me. Only me."

"Well, that just can't happen."

She said this with the distinct lack of filter that kids tend to have. She looked at me, registering the pain in my eyes, and then continued anyway.

"Well, then he can't possibly be with you. He probably thinks you already moved on. He will probably fall in love, and when he dies, he will be with her wherever her soul goes."

"I don't want this. I can't stand this, watching him love someone new."

"Oh," She said, tilting her head down, finally getting it. "Does he really love someone new?"

"I mean... I don't think so.... not yet, at least. I think he still loves me for now. But I see him falling for someone.... What am I doing? Telling you everything! What about you? What's going on with you?"

"Sita, I live in an elevator. I promise you I have nothing cool to talk about. Well, there is still one way you could be with him."

I looked at her. I found during my time as a ghost that ghosts are kind of like really bad co-workers. Everyone knows different parts of how the business works but never gets together to tell each other. So, I looked at her excitedly. Maybe she had a new ghost rule or hack that would help me.

"Well, he could die." She could tell I was shocked.

"I mean if he died right now. He could be murdered. Picture someone rigged this elevator to just fall and explode." She said, making a motion with her hands to show.

"You would be free to carry on with him as ghosts forever. Free to be whoever you want." She paused, "Besides be alive, obviously."

"I don't want him to be killed, Kyra," I said, desperately trying to determine how serious her threat was. I feared again how much power she actually had.

"It was just a suggestion." She said, shrugging her shoulders. "You shouldn't complain anyway. One day you'll be free. I'll forever be in this elevator."

"What if someone tried to save you?"

"It's too late. All I can do now is hope more people get killed." I looked at her concerned and then replied,

"Why would you say that?"

"The more people that are killed, the more friends I will have."

The elevator's buttons lit up, and the elevator started to

move. Ash let out a huge sigh as if he had been holding his breath. I felt relieved, too, only because I didn't know how to talk to Kyra sometimes. I felt as though she was losing herself, but if I couldn't even save myself, I had no idea how to save her too. Kyra jumped up.

"Dang it, I thought it was going to be longer." I shot her a look. But before she could ravel up a terrible excuse, the elevator doors opened, and I waved at Kyra nervously on our way out.

The rest of the day was pretty ordinary, or at least as a day for a dead girl can be. I sat next to Ash as he took movie ticket after movie ticket, and I suddenly understood why he hated his job so much. It felt like I was living the same day over and over again.

I looked for ghosts whenever the front door would open, wondering how many of us there were. I was always hoping I would find more like me. I understood Kyra's dark thoughts in the elevator a bit. I just wanted another ghost to be living the same life as me, someone who could relate to me just a bit more than a little girl ghost that was probably 100 years old. Instead, when a ghost did enter, I hid from them until I knew if they were ok or not. They were rarely ok.

The worst part of work had become the sweet little exchanges between Ash and Emma throughout the day. He delivered her a Coke to the front and gave her a wink. She waved and smiled as she walked by him to the restroom. What brought them joy made me sick. By the end of the day, the villains upped their sickening game as we walked out to leave. Emma was taking a phone call, and I was relieved I wouldn't have to hear her voice again. But before we reached the elevator, it sang into our ears.

"Wait, Ash, what are you doing tonight?"

They arranged another date, and I felt implications lingering in the air.

One of the few benefits of being a ghost was that I could cry whenever I wanted, and lately, that meant all the time.

"So, what time works best for you, Ash?"

She asked in the voice that could soothe the world but made me shiver. At that moment, I saw Detective Brady's name come up on his phone. Ash saw it, too,

"6:30," He said as he rushed out like he wasn't interested, even though he was deeply interested. We walked to the car a few moments later when the phone rang again, and Ash picked up.

"Sure, I'll be home in 20."

He said before hanging up. We made it home within 5 minutes, and he laid on the bed until the doorbell rang.

Detective Ronaldson took a seat in a tan chair, and Ash sat across from him on the couch.

"Thank you for seeing me again. As the investigation unfolds, I may come by from time to time. You aren't a suspect. But you're the only person who may be able to help us solve this."

"It's not an issue," Ash replied coolly.

He shifted in his seat, "What do you need?"

"We have a couple new things to discuss." He said as he pulled a file out from his suitcase.

"We can start with this."

He pulled out a picture of a piece of the cover of my journal. My journal was bright blue with daisies all around it. But this was only a piece of the cover that looked as if it had been torn off.

"Do you recognize it?"

Ash leaned over and looked over the picture.

"That could be her journal."

Detective Ronaldson wrote diligently on a notepad.

"We found it in one of her jean pockets."

I remembered.

I remembered pulling out my journal from the drawer in our room. I remembered wanting to get away and take a walk to somewhere secluded so that I could journal. I was so confused about my age. I was only 18, and the whole world was asking me what I would do with the rest of my life.

"Any idea why this would have been in one of her pockets?"

"No, sir." He said cockily, staring the Detective straight in the eye. "Any reason you haven't brought this up before?"

"We don't lay all our cards down at once, son." He continued, "Ok, well, the next thing I want to ask about is this." He said, placing down a picture of a bag of what looked like drugs.

"This was found in her left shoe."

Ash stood and looked closely at the picture. "I don't know what that is."

"It's heroin, Ash. Did Sita have an issue with drugs?"

"What the fuck?"

He took the picture and looked at it closer. Then he threw it at the Detective.

"I don't believe you, and I don't want to talk anymore today."

The Detective picked the picture up and put it back in the suitcase.

"Ash, if Sita was doing drugs, it could explain some things. We have a drug dealer in custody for heroin intent to sell and his girlfriend's attempted murder. She was an 18-year-old heroin addict."

Ash sat back down and let his head drop into his hands. I put my hand on his back and rubbed it as if I were comforting him. He scratched at his back like there was a bug.

"I don't know."

I pulled my hand back; I couldn't believe it. He didn't know? He didn't know? He knew I would never touch drugs.

Then I remembered myself. I didn't know either. Why would I have had drugs on me? I didn't do heroin. I had to remember. But I was scared to remember too. I knew that if they discovered my murderer if I was there when they solved it. I would spend the rest of the murderer's time haunting them. My best hope was that my murderer would get the death penalty. Maybe they would die, and I would be free.

"Look, Ash,"

The Detective said as he neatly lined up all his papers perfectly into his folder. "We want to solve this. We are going to want to talk to you again, but until then, I need you to think. Think about the last times that you saw her. Think about anything different or strange within the last couple months."

"I will. "Ash responded without looking up.

"That's all I need for now." Detective Ronaldson grabbed his stuff and left the house.

Ash went straight to his room and lay face down on the bed, his face deep in the soft sheets. He reached out for my green cardigan and buried his face into it. He just laid there for a few minutes until I tried to lay next to him and the bed slightly shook. He jumped up and rubbed his eyes. I could see the exhaustion in his eyes and the deep and dark circles beginning to form underneath them, and I wondered how much longer I could afford to be so selfish.

He got into the shower and got ready for his date, as I just watched. I watched him take off his shirt and change, and I wanted nothing more than to be the person he was getting ready for. I tried not to move much. As much as I didn't want him to go on this date, I also didn't want to scare him anymore and didn't want to make things worse. As he put his rough hands through his now dull golden-brown hair to style it, the doorbell rang and made us both jump.

But, to my surprise, he didn't rush. He sighed and washed his hands. Then he walked over to the white nightstand by our, by his bed. He gently traced the heart that we had carved in with his fingers. He opened the drawer and pulled out a picture of us. I had shoulder-length black curly hair and a small yellow top with black pants.

I was curled into his body, and we both beamed with wide smiles. Behind us was a large aquarium tank with beautiful fishes stopped in motion for the picture. On our first anniversary, we had gone to the aquarium and had become children again in awe of nature. Seeing the picture reminded me of what Ash had been like before all of this. His smile and love for me so immense. I felt like I hadn't seen that Ash in so long.

One day I realized I would remember Ash after me more than I remembered him with me.

He gently guided his thumb along with me in the picture, and the doorbell rang again. Still, in no hurry, he held the picture to his chest and closed his eyes. I didn't try to touch him, and I'm not quite sure why.

13

Done

Ash opened the old white door that had paint peeling like it was shedding its skin. There stood Emma. I wanted to not care what she looked like. I wanted to close my eyes and hide in the corner the whole time. But sometimes, our human instinct to hurt ourselves far outweighs our instinct to save ourselves.

She looked perfect, aside from the slightly annoyed look on her face, that I assumed came from him taking his time to answer the door. Her long and vivid chestnut hair was curled away from her face, allowing me to see what I had dreaded. She was still beautiful. Don't get me wrong, I believed she could have really used a couple of makeup wipes, and I wondered what she would look like without the exaggerated eyelashes that burst out from her face. But I knew she was still beautiful.

Neither of them said anything for a moment; she waited like she expected an invite or an apology. But he just looked at her, no, it was much worse than that. He was looking into her until she broke my rising self-pity with her voice.

"You look nice, Ash." She said as she shifted to a giant and perfect white smile. Once she knew she couldn't control him with pouts.

Ash looked down at his worn in converse and deep blue jeans, "Oh, thanks, I really went all out." He said with a wink. A wink. My wink. That was how he used to wink at me. I rolled my eyes and walked back towards the worn-out black couch.

He opened the door wider and let her in.

"Here, take a seat."

He said, pointing to the living room.

"I'll get you a drink, water? Wine?"

"I'll take wine, thank you." She said as she walked in.

Then, you will not believe this shit. She came in and sat right where I was. She sat in her gemmed up blue jeans, and she did it with a smirk on her face. I immediately stood up. I was tired of this already. I got right into her perfectly mani-cured face, and she looked down, but I told myself that I was talking to her like we were both living. Because sometimes you have to pretend to survive.

"Listen here bitch. He is mine. Ash is my boyfriend. Until he dies, I'm stuck with him."

I stood back up, for a moment, taken aback by what I had just said. Was that really how I felt? Stuck with him?

"Well, I'm not giving up yet, lady. If I can scare him, I bet I can scare you too."

I went around the room with fists tight, hitting everything I could, hoping to make a noise, but nothing happened. I was desperately pushing buttons on the TV remote when Ash returned with a drink and handed it to Emma. She smiled at him as she took the drink, and I thought I saw him blush.

"So, today turned out being a bit different than I thought it would," Ash said in a softer voice that was normally reserved for me. "I wanted to make a whole romantic dinner with candles and flowers."

She smiled shyly, and I felt the awkward mood of two people getting to know each other. A feeling I was grateful they were feeling too.

"I got pulled out to ... to do some stuff, and I couldn't get it all. I could still make you dinner if you'd like." He pulled his shirt down a bit, "Or I could just take you somewhere."

"I would love to have you cook me dinner." She said sweetly and shyer than she ever was at work. She was smoother than I ever was. Ash was always the smooth and collected one in our relationship. But something here was different. He was more flustered than her, and everything she did felt like she had been meant to do it.

"Ok." he hopped up with excitement. "I just need like 20 minutes, if that's ok. Do you need anything?"

"No, that sounds great. I'll just hang out." She said, pulling out her phone almost as proof that she would be fine for 20 minutes.

He got up and went back towards the kitchen. I just sat down next to Emma with my arms closed tight. I spent the first ten minutes staring in front of me as she scrolled through her phone. I didn't know what to say or do. A part of me wanted to retreat to another part of the house, to hide in a corner like Ash's grandfather always did.

I stood back up and started hitting things again. I brushed my hand through the curtains, slammed the door, tried to push over a lamp, anything. She just played on her phone like nothing was happening. I began screaming. I stood in the middle of the room and screamed as loud as I could. For a moment, I cried, hopeless as always. I couldn't stop scaring Ash, but I couldn't even budge anything to scare Emma. Then I stopped, straightened myself back up, and looked at her.

"I'm not hopeless," I said as a walked to her.

I began hitting her, hoping she could feel anything. Pretending I could feel my fist hitting her flesh. I hit her for a couple of minutes. If I had been human, it would have been the beating of a lifetime. But, as a ghost, I saw her shift in her seat just a bit, and that's it. I stopped, tired, hopeless, and fell into the chair across from her that Ash usually sat in. When I sat, she put her phone down and looked up.

"Are you done yet, Sita?"

I froze. I stared at her as if I were the one who saw a ghost. I looked all around me; this must have been some kind of mistake. My anger had grown since I died. I felt angry all the time. But, in this brief moment, I didn't. I felt like a child, confused, and lost. After all my yelling and hitting, I couldn't say one word.

"I'm sorry you're going through this; it must be really hard."

She said, now speaking to me in the soft voice that made me agonize but also feel slightly soothed. I leaned in closer.

"Are you talking to me?" I almost whispered.

She smiled sweetly, "I am. I haven't been candid."

She looked towards the kitchen and then back at me. She lowered her voice to a whisper.

"Well, I didn't lie to you; I just didn't let you know I could see you. I'm a medium. I have been my whole life. I didn't want to tell you. I didn't want you to be mad at me. But obviously, we are way past that." She said, looking at me with a very brief and passing annoyed look.

I wanted to yell and scream at her. But I was too shocked and maybe scared.

"I like Ash. I really do. He deserves happiness, Sita. You think I don't recognize the exhaustion in his eyes? You're hurting him. Let him move on. I can help you. I can help you find your murderer."

I continued to stare at her. I could feel my eyes popping out of my face. Before I could answer, or more likely, before I could continue to stare at her silently and awkwardly, Ash walked back in. He held two plates in the way only a previous server could and set them on the dining room table.

She winked at me, got up, and walked to the table. "Oh my, it looks amazing, Ash." She said, sitting down in front of the spaghetti dish I had taught him to make.

I sat in the same seat; I didn't move. I couldn't go over there, knowing she could see me and hear me. This changed everything. I felt embarrassed. I felt betrayed. But mostly, I felt guilty. I felt guilty now that I knew someone knew what I was doing. I knew I was selfish. I knew I was keeping Ash from living his life. I was doing everything I could to make him realize I was here. So, I sat there. I let them have their dinner, let them laugh, and talk and become closer with every word they shared. While they did, I just stared into the space she once sat.

I barely noticed when they got up from dinner and went upstairs to watch a movie. I also didn't want to. I was comfortable here. But, for the first time in a long time, I was actually thinking about him first. I wanted him to have a night. She was right. He deserved to be happy. It was like I had completely forgotten that. The more I lived in a world where no one was keeping me accountable, the less I was doing the right thing.

When they came walking back down the stairs late at night, I wondered if I had imagined all of it. She looked straight at me and smiled as she came down, reassuring me that it was real. After he closed the door and she left, he leaned up against it, and smiled, smiled in a profound way that I hadn't seen since before I died.

He went to sleep. I laid next to him and just watched him all night. He woke up and looked around like he felt it. I didn't run and hide like I normally did; I stayed. I didn't care if I scared him, not right now. Not when I was thinking of doing everything I could to never see him again.

The next day, Ash didn't have work, and I was grateful. I did what I did about once a week when I was living. I laid in bed all day thinking, pouting, and crying. It made me miss eating and being able to choose what I wanted to watch on TV. But the pouting and crying were even better when I didn't have those distractions anyway.

For some reason, I felt everything changed. Emma was the first person to really call me out on what I was doing. Dave wasn't helpful, and there was no guarantee I would ever get to see him again. As much as I liked talking to Kyra, I also knew deep down that something was wrong there.

She was dark. I felt it. Maybe, she wasn't dark and evil when she was alive. Maybe she really was just a happy little girl who was in the wrong place at the wrong time. But maybe it was this, being a ghost. Being a ghost for so many years made her dark and evil, and she didn't even see it. Where would I be in a few years? Would I spend 20 years with Ash? What if I grew angrier and darker every year? Would this be the rest of his life?

Late at night, I sat up thinking because I couldn't sleep. It was the biggest torture in the afterlife; there was no end to my thought. Ash stayed up because I accidentally turned the TV on twice while dealing with my dead emotions. At around 1 am, we both heard the door open. Theresa and Tony came stumbling in and yelling like a party had just begun. We both listened as we heard Theresa using the wall as a crutch to get into the bedroom.

Ash got up and went downstairs. Tony was drinking a beer at the kitchen table, leaning back in the chair like a child in school. Ash sat down.

"Ash! Buddy, son of mine. How are you doing?" Tony slurred out lovingly. It was out of his character. But just because he was often angry drunk didn't mean a happy drunk didn't exist. His mother and Tony were like a minefield, you might survive it when you take a step, or you might explode.

"Hey, Tony. I'm doing fine. Can I tell you something?"

I felt jealous of Tony for the first time. I wanted Ash to tell me something so badly. I supposed that Tony would be a perfect therapist for Ash. Ash was not emotionally mature enough to really disclose how he was feeling to a therapist. He would be too scared of what they might reveal. Tony, on the other hand, would not remember anything Ash said in the morning. In fact, he wouldn't remember ever having a nice conversation with Ash.

"Of course, man," Tony said, taking another sip of his beer.

"I think we have a ghost in the house," Ash said, tying up his flannel pants around his waist.

"A ghost." He took another sip of the beer and smiled. "I don't believe in ghosts, buddy. What we can see is real. Do you see a ghost?" He said, pointing around.

"No, but it messes with me constantly. I can't sleep."

"Naw, man. You can't sleep because you're still here. Living off your mom and me. You would be happier getting your own place." He pulled out some cigarettes and lit one up, blowing the smoke in Ash's direction, and continued, "I mean, at least we got that chick out of here, but you're next." He pointed the cigarette at Ash.

"Tony, I pay all the bills. If it wasn't for me, you guys would be on the streets."

"I got a few side businesses here. If you ever need something, you let me know."

"Ok," Ash said, standing up and pushing in the chair. He got as much listening out of Tony as was probably possible. "Night, Tony."

14

Hope

The next day when Ash went to work, I knew that Emma was my only hope. We got into the elevator and rode it down to the staff lounge. Kyra perked up when I entered, and I felt guilty for all the bad things I had thought about her.

"Sita!"

"Kyra, how can I help you?"

She gave me an angry look that only children can't at least partially conceal.

"You can't. I am forever here. You already know that."

I stood in silence, hopeless and unhelpful.

"But you could be." she continued.

Then a smile once again reached across her face, and she walked up towards Ash, staring up at him.

"That's why I told you if we can just kill this one, you could be free."

"I just wish we could put you somewhere new," I said sadly as the door opened to the lounge, and we walked out.

After the elevator closed, I stared at the door, wishing I

could help her. I had a new kindness about me today that I hadn't felt in a long time. A renewed energy that reminded me of me before my death. I think it was knowing that I was finally about to do the right thing.

When Ash went upstairs, he went and stood at the theater's door, where he would be collecting tickets. I walked across the lobby to where Emma sat, playing on her phone because there wasn't a line. I was happy to see she was alone, and we would really have time to speak.

I walked up to her and stood by her side. She didn't look at me, and I wondered again whether I imagined everything. But she turned just for a moment and smiled at me, then looked forward again.

"Sorry, I can't look." She whispered. "One of the hardest things about being a medium is not getting locked up for being crazy."

As she said this, another coworker walked into the ticket booth and took a seat a couple of feet away. It was Alec, a petite 16-year-old who looked like he could be 12. She smiled at him as he sat.

"The meanager said a rush will be coming soon, so she wanted me up here with you." He shrugged and pulled out his own phone.

Emma pulled a notepad to the side I was standing on and wrote. She was one of those girls with perfect handwriting. Big and wonderful curves in each letter as she wrote.

Did you think about what I said?

"I did. I'm ready. I'm ready to haunt my murderer." I looked back at Ash, who was helping an older woman to a seat in the lobby.

"He deserves happiness; you're right. I don't know if you're his happiness. If you hurt him, I will find a way to come for you. "

She smirked; I think knowing that I was completely bluffing.

I will need your help, trying to find who killed you. There is a chance we won't be able to find him.

"Well, I'm at least ready to start trying."

What do you know?

As she finished writing, a couple came up to buy tickets, and she quickly flipped the pad over so they wouldn't see her notes. I collected my thoughts and thought about everything I knew as the rush Alec had mentioned arrived. When it ended, Alec gave Emma a head nod and walked away.

"Ok, so here is what I know," I said, ready to explode. She put a one-second finger up and pulled her purse out. She pulled out a small mirror and reapplied her lip gloss. For that moment, I felt hate for her again, a longing to do something to her, to ask Kyra for advice.

She slowly flipped the notebook over and to a new page.

Ok go ahead.

"I fell off a bridge, or I guess I was pushed. I can't remember. But the police are saying it was murder. My keys and pepper spray were missing, and my car was in the lot. They found a piece of my journal's cover but not the journal itself."

Emma was writing each point down.

"Oh," I said hesitantly. "And they found a bag of heroin in my shoe." She looked up at me like I had just offered her heroin.

I shrugged, and she wrote it down as the last bullet.

"Ok," she said with a sigh.

"Hey Emma, wondering if you brought lunch?"

Emma jumped as Ash appeared on the other side of her without either of us noticing. She fumbled over the notebook to close it, in what was the most awkward action I had seen.

He smiled, "Writing about me or something?"

She pulled her fingers through her hair for a seductive recovery.

"Well, that is none of your business, Mr. Ash."

"Lunch or you writing about me?"

She smirked, "Writing, lunch is most definitely your business. Why don't we take it in 30?"

"Perfect," He said.

Then he pulled from his pocket a small rose he must have picked from the bushes surrounding the theatre. She blushed and took it to smell it. He smiled and walked back to where he collected tickets.

I fake puked.

"Well, one day, if we do this right. You won't have to watch all this."

She pulled the notebook back out, flipped the page, and began writing to me again.

Heroin?

"I don't do heroin. I never would. It has to be connected to my murderer somehow."

She had a look like a lightbulb had gone off in her head.

Suspects?

"It could be no one or anyone." I said, looking down, ashamed. "No one is that close to me, but I'm the type of person anyone could hate. People I know, though. Well, Ash, but he was working. He has a tight alibi. Plus, he would never, and I've watched him grieve." She had a look of relief as I said this.

"My aunt was technically my guardian. She always hated me even though I never asked her for anything. I don't see why she'd kill me because she wouldn't have any reason to see me in the first place, and she can't keep a secret to save her life. I guess Theresa, Ash's mother."

I noticed that I had been instinctively just explaining why no one I knew could have done this. But I had nothing to say for Theresa, nothing strong at least.

"She never liked me, but it wouldn't be her. That would be crazy. Plus, we have to remember heroin! That makes me almost sure it wasn't Theresa or anyone else I know. Which leads to the last, the detective mentioned some drug dealer."

She diligently wrote as I talked way too fast. When I was finished, she looked at the clock, 10 minutes till our date with Ash.

Maybe next time, let's talk about what you last remember? You know it gets busy here after lunch, so spend a day or two thinking about it.

I shook my head. It was laughable how someone that at one time, I thought of as the enemy now felt like my guidance counselor.

My guidance counselor.

My guidance counselor.

I remembered talking to my guidance counselor. But if Ash was working, it had to have been a Saturday when I was killed. I wouldn't have seen my guidance counselor on a Saturday.

My guidance counselor was Mr. Kelly. He was young,

maybe in his twenties. With hip hair that he wore in a small bun on his head. The more I pictured him, the more I pictured last seeing him. I remembered going into his too-small room and sitting on his faded maroon chair that looked like it had seen years of crying teens.

He asked me if I had a journal.

I thought of this as Ash and Emma had their sweet lunch.

When they returned, it did indeed get busy. But I sat next to Ash's booth, and I perked up when I saw a ghost wander in. Seemingly from what I could only imagine was a hundred years ago. It was a young boy about my age wearing tan pajamas that look like they had been hand sewn. Before he entered, I watched him look through the movies at the front booth. To my amusement, I noticed Emma glance over at him while she was working. I didn't know how she hid it from me at all in hindsight.

Then he walked back through the lobby. He smiled when he saw me, and I got up.

"Well, hello."

"Hi, I'm Sita. Who are you?"

This was more social than I ever was while I was alive. I guess that was part of the perk of being dead. When you can't talk to people very often, it reminds you how sweet the joy of a conversation is. Not just how lovely it is, but how needed it is. Our souls, dead or alive, thirst for interaction.

"I'm James. What do you think about this movie Spider-man? Should I see it?"

I was taken aback, expecting someone scared or evil like the other ghosts I had met and confused by the question.

"I mean, I don't know."

"You haven't seen it?!"

"No," I said, suddenly a bit embarrassed.

He laughed and began slightly jumping on his heels.

"You attached to this guy or this place?"

"This guy. Are you attached?"

"Nope, followed my mama for about 20 years till she passed. Now I just live my life. Well... you know what I mean. Now, let me get this straight, you are stuck, coming here, to the movie theater, and you're not watching movies?"

I shrugged, "I guess I never thought about it."

"Well, you been missing a whole world." He put out his arm.

"Now, let's go see about this Spiderman film, ma'am."

I looked at Ash and Emma, almost like I would have looked at my parents. I smiled and took his arm and followed him to the theater.

Watching the movie felt very strange, in the best possible way. It was the first time I felt like I was able to escape Ash's boring life. I felt like I was exploring and seeing something new. I was thrilled with the endless possibilities.

I thought about all the movies playing right now and how I would watch all of them. I also felt sad for all the ones I had missed. I was so consumed with Ash and Emma and what I wanted that I didn't see a simple joy that was right there in front of me. When the movie was over, we walked out. James tilted his head to me.

"That was lovely. Thanks for joining me, miss. I've got to be going. I've got plans with a friend to jump a plane to Spain. But I come by occasionally. I'm sure I'll see you again."

I thanked him a bit too excitedly.

I suddenly wondered if I had just gone on a date, and I did instinctively what all girls do. I ran to the bathroom to see how I looked when we were together. I looked the same. The same as I always did. My grungy clothes and wild black hair. My skin free of makeup and any real effort. I tried to look at myself in a new way. I tried to look at myself as he may have. I was pretty, I knew it deep down, but instead, I focused on how I wished I had died wearing a pretty dress.

I remembered how happy he seemed, and I felt hope. Remembered he said friend, another thing I hadn't thought of. I guess when you get through haunting or protecting, freedom could mean so many things. People always say to live in the present. Don't think about the past or the future too much. Sometimes the past or the future actually is the safest place to be. This wasn't my forever; it was just a piece of my story. Even if and when I moved on to my murderer, it was only while they are living.

There was hope.

I walked out of the bathroom and looked to Ash, who was also looking at the clock. I had some time. So, I went into the nearest theater and watched part of a movie in there too. For the first time, I was disappointed when I was being pulled towards the elevator to go back to the staff room.

15

Remember

When I got to the elevator, my first instinct was to tell Kyra all about my new discovery and the boy who came to the theater. But I stopped myself just in time when I remembered those simple joys were things she could never have. Suddenly, my hope was joined by another foreign feeling, gratefulness. So, I didn't say anything, and she was busy twirling in circles anyway. Ash grabbed his jacket and went back into the elevator, where Kyra was now sitting, trying to get rid of her dizziness.

"Hey, Kyra. Do you remember how you died?"

"Kinda. I remember going down this elevator when it used to be a bank. Someone was in here with me, and I think they choked me." She said, pressing her hand around her neck.

"Why do you think I can't remember?"

The doors opened, and I looked back at her.

"It's normal. Some ghost once told me it's just like humans. Sometimes they forget the real bad stuff."

I smiled at her and waved goodbye as the door shut again, and Ash and I went home for the day.

Before Ash got out of his car, the phone rang. It was Detective Ronaldson. Ash answered it and stayed in the car to chat as he noticed his mother's faded blue Volkswagen sat uncomfortably at the house. I was relieved he spoke to the Detective through the Bluetooth in the car, for once making me feel involved.

"Hello, is this Ash?"

"Yes. Did you find them?"

"Well, I can't say that. No. But, I can give an update. We are looking into three different suspects. One we have an eye on rather closely. Have you seen the news lately?"

"I don't watch the news."

When I was alive, Ash and I would watch the news together every morning. I wondered if he was too scared to watch it alone now. Too terrified of what they might be saying about me.

"We have a suspect in custody for serial killing. He came from California. Do you recognize the name, Elias?"

"No."

"Well, his suspected victims are all around the same age as Sita. The method of murder is a bit different. So, we would need to know why the change. But one big thing I am looking into is the heroin. He often lured his victims in with drug addiction. When did Sita begin her heroin addiction?"

"Is that what you called for?"

"It is one of the reasons."

"Look, I'm not as dumb as you guys fuckin think I am."

Ash was obviously sick of Detective Ronaldson. I was too.

He never seemed to be very helpful or respectful to Ash at all. Ash was suffering. I'd seen it non-stop. I was living it. But somehow, it seemed like the Detective only tried to make Ash say whatever he wanted to hear. The problem is, the death of a loved one was like dying yourself, only without any of the relief from living.

"I already told you Sita wasn't doing heroin. I don't know why the heroin was there. But if all you're doing is determining her heroin addiction, then you aren't even on the right track."

"Look, I know it's frustrating, Ash, but if you want this to ever be solved–"

"I want you to find the murderer. If it's Elias, great. I want him to die or be in prison forever. But find out yourself, it's not my job to solve this fuckin murder, and you don't even listen to me anyway. Call me when you have the killer."

He hung up and sat in the car for another moment before taking a deep breath and going inside.

He grabbed a book from the small bookcase in the living room. It was a book I gave him for Christmas. It meant he was thinking of me, which made me feel guilty for still thinking about the movies I saw that day. He shouted out for his mother, who he could hear fumbling in the kitchen, "Mom, can you get me a water?"

He sat on the couch and started reading. I went to where the remote sat next to it. I started pushing buttons on it. I was suddenly obsessed with the idea of experiencing new things. It turned on, and Ash jumped as he looked up and stared at the screen.

Theresa entered from the kitchen wobbling left and right,

with a glass of water in her hand. She looked at the TV and then at Ash.

"Well, which is it, Ash? Are you reading or watching TV?"

He snapped out of his fear as she barely managed to set the water down next to him without spilling. "Thanks, mom, I'm uh. Neither." He said, turning off the TV and putting the book down.

"You doing ok, Ash?"

"Ya, I'm fine, mom."

"Any news from the police?"

"They are trying to link it to a serial killer."

"You wouldn't have to be a serial killer to want to kill that messy girl."

He snapped a look at his mother, probably the type of look a mother would usually give a son.

She raised her hands up in surrender, then looked down at her tight orange dress and began straightening it.

"Well, I hope they solve it. I know it would make you feel better."

He lowered his head, less combative but still uninterested.

"I'm going to be leaving town for a couple days."

"What for this time?"

"A romantic trip with that dreamy Tony."

"Ok, whatever." He said and handed her back the water. "This is the water you asked for."

Then he went upstairs to his room, satisfied that he got her to have some water. He spent the rest of the time online looking for information about demons. (Yep, we upgraded to him thinking I'm a demon now) But, I had the best night I have had since dying. I sat there replaying in my head everything that had happened in the movie I saw. Every emotion, every color, every scene was thought of in 50 different ways. Something new.

It wasn't until Ash's obnoxious siren alarm went off that I remembered that I was supposed to have spent the evening recalling my last memories. You would think that the Detective's implications about a serial killer would have left me up all night thinking about it.

When I was alive, I couldn't help but concentrate on all the terrible and bitter things in my life. Whenever anything good happened, it was like I couldn't see it at all. But now that I was dead, I was concentrating more on the happy things, even though there were so many less of them. The movies, watching a movie with a boy, well, it was the first good thing I felt in a long time, and I couldn't help but feel it, live it, and be it.

I looked at Ash as he got ready, and I felt that maybe I was doing the wrong thing for a moment. What terrible harm was I really causing him? Could it possibly be any worse than me having to follow around some serial killer until he dies? I had a chance at some freedom here. As long as he was working at the movie theater, I could go in every day and watch as many movies as I wanted. Things just didn't feel so bad. Especially since I was dealing with his relationship with Emma better, was it selfish for me to think about what would be best for me?

Then I remembered the look of fear on his face when the TV had turned on. As if it was a sign from below, I walked back and forth, pondering my options. When one of my footsteps was suddenly audible, I heard it loudly myself and stopped walking mid-step. He turned around, and I thought I saw a tear form in his eyes.

I stopped walking and sat right there on the floor to not make another noise. I had precious little time. I couldn't tell Emma that thoughts of Spider-Man had stopped me from solving my murder. So far, what I had was the guidance counselor. I remembered him asking about my journal at school. But I couldn't remember anything past that.

I knew I was at school. It was finals, about two weeks before graduation. I remembered the week before studying at our local library. I was drinking five coffees a day and living off burritos that Ash would drop off to me. That week was clear.

There were late nights in Ash's arms as we both held books and studied. The staying up till 4 am, Ash and I talking about our future. I didn't feel like any of that was very helpful. I remembered back as far as I wanted. That wasn't the problem.

Ok, focus.

Finals.

Guidance Counselor.

There had to be something else. A kiss, I remembered Ash pulling me in so tight after he finished finals and kissing me so hard. Like words of hope for our future could have been communicated through that kiss alone.

I had nothing else.

When we got to Ash's work, I asked Kyra if she knew about the medium who worked there. She coyly smiled like she had gotten away with something, and I immediately realized that she had always known about Emma.

When we got upstairs and Ash walked to his post at the

stand, I felt something was different. I looked at him from all angles. I had been so wrapped up in Spider-Man, and then in trying to remember that I hadn't been paying much attention to him at all. His phone buzzed, and I got in close to read the text. It was from Emma. We both looked up at the ticket booth. And saw Emma turned towards him in her chair and wave, and then she turned back around, as a family arrived to get tickets.

You ok?

Ya just got an unsettling text this morning.

What do you mean?

I don't want to bring you into it.

I want to be in it.

It was from a blocked number, it said Sita wasn't who I thought she was. Just makes me scared, I mean, what if it's right?

I'm sorry, Ash. Is there anything I can do? No way we can trace the number? You should call the police and show them.

Ya, your right. Want to come over tonight?

Sure, maybe I could make you dinner this time?

I'd love that.

I walked over to where Emma sat. The nice thing about still being around was that I could still keep them separate a bit if I wanted to.

"Can't you wait to do this shit with him until we figure this out?"

She smirked but didn't look at me.

"Look, I didn't see the text he talked about, but it has to be a prank. I think we should focus on some things I remembered. I remember parts of the day before. I remember it was our last day. We were finishing finals. At the end of the day,

I went to my counselor. He asked about my notebook, but I don't remember why."

She pulled the same notebook she had kept our notes in yesterday from her purse, turned the page, and wrote what I had told her.

Then she wrote.

You don't know why a counselor would want you to have a journal?

She looked at me passive-aggressively and then circled the word counselor.

"Ok, sure, but I have to wonder what he wanted me to write about. Why he wanted me to have it?"

You trust him?

"Ya, why not? Didn't know him that well. Sometimes he would let me sit in his office when I had a panic attack, talked to me when my grades fell behind, and about college options."

What about the day?

"I've tried ok, but I can't remember anything."

Well, what do you normally do on a Saturday?

"Well, Ash often worked on Saturdays, so I usually worked out and tended to my small garden."

Why would you have gone to the bridge?

"Sometimes, I would go there to think."

This brought back a memory, my pink tennis shoes walking on the bridge's faded light-colored wood boards. That's all I saw, though. It wasn't enough to tell Emma about, but it was a vital reminder that I could do this. That somewhere in my dead brain were the memories I needed.

16

Joy

After I spoke with Emma that day, I walked straight to the movie theaters, past Ash, without even looking at him. This felt like a breakup. Only I hadn't realized we were breaking up until very recently. I was feeling stronger, less attached. I was letting go of what he had already let go of.

The only problem was that it was like the type of breakup where you still work with your ex. I had to see him every day, whether I wanted to or not. Every time I looked at him, it shot a love and hate wave through my whole body. Every time I began to heal, his eyes brought me right back to the beginning. But every day I was making a new choice, I was moving without him.

I went to the left and found about five theaters. I read the titles above them and chose one that sounded like a children's film. I watched that movie and felt child-like afterward. Children's movies had a way of reminding me how light and funny the world really was. After that, I went from theater to theater and caught whatever parts of the movies I could, feeling relief after each one.

Towards the end of the day, I wanted to save the last two movies I hadn't seen yet for another day. I walked out to the main lobby where Ash was. I sat down on a small black bench directly behind him. Movies were such a simple pleasure, a simple joy that I completely forgot I had any access to. I wondered about the other simple joys that I was ignoring. I heard the music that played in the lobby. I guess I really heard it the whole time, but for the first time since I died, I felt it.

I stood up from the bench. I looked around at the people entering the theater and exiting. I felt embarrassed about what I was about to do. But I reminded myself that no one could see me.

I danced. I spent the next thirty minutes jumping, twirling, and moving with the new pop music that blasted through the lobby. I danced through people, into theaters, and finally dropped down next to Ash. I smiled. I was nothing but negative since I died. Suddenly, I was becoming someone I recognized. I was becoming more alive than I was when I was alive.

When we got into the elevator to leave for the day, I smiled at Kyra. She looked like I attacked her with the smile and even stepped back. "What's with you?"

"I've just been feeling better lately, that's all. How can I make you feel better?"

"You can't."

I sighed, knowing deep down that she was right, and once again, it felt selfish to be happy. I was lucky not to be trapped in a place like she was. I was lucky not to be haunting my murderer yet. I was lucky to experience joy, even if it was just for the smallest moment. I decided I would never forget Kyra. I hoped that someday I would somehow save her.

We left and went home for the day. Ash brought out the book he was reading and curled up under our comforter in the room to read. He pulled my plaid cardigan in close. I sat next to him. He felt the bed shift a bit but acted like he didn't. I just stared at him, then I laid onto his chest and spoke with him as if he could hear me. I had been able to talk to so few people and so few ghosts. No one I was actually close to. I just needed Ash for a bit.

"I am feeling a lot better, Ash. I hope I feel better wherever else I go too. I am trying to leave you, Ash. Not that I want to, I want to be with you forever. But I know this is what is best for you, and that's all I want. You know I love you, and I know you love me. It's funny, I'm with you all the time, Ash, but somehow, I miss you so much I can't explain it. I know this is it for us, too. When you die, you'll move on. But, when I am free from this sentence, I still don't move on. I stay here. The only way we will be together ever again is if you are murdered."

I looked up at him. I slid my hand gently across his deep brown cheek.

"And I don't want that for you. I don't want this for you. You are my soulmate, Ash. But sometimes you can't have your soulmate. One day I'll find peace in this, but never, I'll never forget this."

Just then, his mother stumbled into his room, her hair straying from the normal tight curls on her head and her dress slightly to the side. Clearly drunk.

"Ash! You're here."

Ash didn't look up from his book.

"I thought you were out of town with Tony?"

"Oh ya, I am!! I need my bathing suit. Also, I'm going to take my car with me. Tony drove me here. But we think my car will be better."

Tony peeked his head in. He was clearly drunk, too, and almost fell over. Ash stop looking at his book then and looked Tony square in his eyes or at least as square as he could since Tony's eyes kept moving in different directions.

"Cool, can you get me a glass of water first?" Ash said, looking at his mom after his long and cold stare at Tony.

"Oh, you got it, babay!" She said, and as soon as she walked out the door and to the left to go to the basement.

Ash looked back at Tony, "Hey man, mom said to go meet her on the porch, and she will meet you out there with her car keys."

Over the years, Ash had become quite the professional at tricking drunk people into doing what he needed them to do, which was a convenient skill to have since sometimes he had to trick them into not killing themselves. I assumed, this was what Ash was doing as he jumped up and ran to his mom's room down the hall. She had an older decorated room with a bed decorated with yellow daisies. He checked all the counters and began opening drawers.

He went to the closet and started looking through her coat pockets. Then he stopped, mid-coat search as he pulled keys out of a black down jacket. But they weren't her keys.

Ash stared down at the keys, brushed his hand over the blue puffball I had attached to them. I looked at him in shock. He turned them over and then slid them in his pocket. Theresa was stumbling her way up the stairs with the water.

He quickly searched the other coats, found her keys, and slipped them into his other pocket. He ran out and met his mom on the stairs.

"Here," she said, leaning on the wall with all her weight.

"That's for you, Mom. You said you wanted water."

"Oh, you know how I am sometimes." She shrugged and giggled to herself. "I guess no one's perfect."

"I guess so." He said, satisfied that she still fell for that trick every time.

"Now what did I come here for?"

"You came to get your bathing suit. I called you an Uber. It should be here soon to take you wherever you want to go. Tony is waiting outside."

"Right! Thanks!" She said, stumbling back out the door.

Ash had my keys. They were in his mother's coat. I wondered for a moment why he hadn't already called the police. What if him not calling the police while she was still at the house meant she could get away? Then I thought of his mother. Besides Emma, she was all he had left, but I didn't think he thought of Emma as long term. She was filling a void; what I once hoped was an irreplaceable void.

So, it was just his mom. His mom wasn't a good mom. He knew it too. I, in fact, almost gained too much joy from picturing her in prison myself. But I suppose it didn't make her not his mom. Of all people, I should have been able to recognize the importance of a mother.

All the years I was with Ash, he only had one concern, his mother. I didn't think he worried about us. We felt so definite. Our love came in waves, but he knew the waves would never cease. But, his mother, his love for his mother, came in flames, and he felt in his heart that they could end at any time.

But, if she did something. If she killed me, and he was to reveal it. What then? He would lose anything he had left. It felt so unfair. I collapsed to the side of his bed and put my head back on it, trying to decide what I even wanted him to do. I didn't know if I wanted to know the truth anymore. I didn't know if I wanted him to pick up the phone and call. I leaned forward and looked up at him. He held an intense gaze towards the wall in front of him; his book left open in his process of thought.

I leaned back. I wanted to leave him for his own good. But I guessed that as long as I knew who committed my murder, that was all that mattered. Maybe the cops didn't need to know at all. I could just shift to haunting his mother. Shift to haunting his mother. Wouldn't I still be haunting him since I would be in the house? I suppose I would have to be careful to avoid him.

The thoughts couldn't stop. If I haunted his mother, she would lose it. She wasn't strong enough. Then again, was Ash strong enough?

I got up and went to sit next to Ash. We could figure this out together, even apart. I delicately placed my hand over his and stared at the same wall as him.

"I trust you, Ash." I paused.

"I understand if you don't turn this in to the police." But then a thought occurred to me, and it devastated me all at once. "But what if.... What if she does this again? If she killed me. Isn't she capable of killing someone else?"

I squeezed at his hand and looked down at it. He moved his hand to on top of his book.

I looked away. "I'm sorry."

He jumped up and let the book fall onto the ground. He stared at the bed in fear.

He heard me, or he heard something.

I tried desperately. I lunged at him in a hug and started shouting.

"I love you!"

" I love you!"

Hoping something in what I said would deliver over. But he didn't give any indication.

He took the keys from his pocket and stared at them. He walked back to his mother's room, opened her dirty closet, and slipped them carefully back into her coat.

Maybe I didn't know anything. Maybe there was a reason that he put the keys back. Maybe there was a reason that she had them in the first place. She was very active. Always in the town. She could have found them, and I tried to reassure myself that he would question her about them later. He returned to his room and picked the book back up off the floor. He flipped through it to find his original page. And grabbed a photo of us on a film strip from his desk and put it in as a bookmark.

He pulled out his phone and jumped back onto the bed to lay down, and I curled up next to him. I knew I was pushing it today. Knew I was getting too close to him and could scare him. But, feeling like my time with him was nearing an end, I did it anyway. He just stared at the phone, and then as he held it, Detective Ronaldson's name came across the screen.

Ash threw the phone into the corner of the room, and it fell like a rock in a river.

17

Escape

The next day was a Tuesday. I knew it was a Tuesday only because Ash always worked with Emma on Tuesdays. So, every Tuesday morning, Ash got up just a bit earlier and got ready just a bit more thoroughly.

It was a good Tuesday, though. I sat behind Ash, thinking of something to do when the door opened, and a familiar face walked in. James tipped his old hat in my direction. I got up like a bee just attacked me; I was so excited to see him. So far, in my dead life, James seemed like the only normal ghost I met.

"Hello, miss, thought I'd come say hello."

"Hey, James! It's great to see you. I've watched every movie since you came by the first time."

"Well, perfect then." He held out his arm for me to hold on to. "You will be the best person to decide which flick we should see today."

I put my arm in his, and even though I couldn't feel anything physically, I felt tingles shooting through my body. We stared up at the movie guide directly above Ash. I looked at Ash, and for a moment, I wanted him to know I was there so he could see me with someone else. I wanted him to taste the jealously I was drowning in. I even selected a romantic movie for James and me to watch.

James was cute. Maybe if we were from the same time and we were both alive, we could have really dated. It was the first time I ever thought about love other than with Ash in years. I never imagined a world where Ash and I wouldn't be together.

But I chose a romantic movie because I just wanted to feel something. I wanted to sit next to a boy in a theater and wonder whether he would hold my hand. I didn't like him. I barely knew him. That didn't stop me from hoping that I was still capable of feeling emotions other than jealousy and hopelessness. It was nice. It was nice sitting there and wondering if he liked me.

After the movie, I asked if he wanted to hang out for a bit. He smiled and adjusted his hat. We walked over to one of the small tables in the lobby area. We chose a table with the chairs slightly out already. He pretended to pull the chair out for me and gave me a little wink. Then we both sat down.

"How have you been, Sita?"

I took a deep breath. A simple question like 'How have you been?' is a loaded gun when you haven't been ok.

"I've been ok. Ash has been trying to get rid of me. He did some things in the home that really hurt me." I said.

"I'm so sorry you had to go through that. I hear terrible things. There is an abandoned house here in town that I like to stay at. It's a community of us ghosts. But since there are so many of us, sometimes someone will slip up. So, we get these wackos in at least once a week. They are mostly harmless. They walk around the house and try to get us to talk to them. Sometimes they threaten to cleanse the house. But they never gone through with it. We just stay as quiet as possible and hope one day they will stop coming."

"A community of ghosts?" I said, excitedly flinging one of my curls, "Are there a lot of ghosts?"

"Oh, yes. Good ghosts tend to stay together. There are tons of places where ghost communities exist. Nature is a great place for them. They don't have to worry about scaring people or overthinking. Death is the first place you don't have to worry about any human things."

"Why do you come here, then?" I asked.

"I've always liked new things. I have to see what is new sometimes. That's why I like movies so much. They really give you a picture of something new and how the world is advancing."

I looked down and then glanced at the elevator door.

"What about the bad ghosts?"

James looked around nervously.

"Do you have any bad ghosts?"

"I don't know. I think I for sure saw one at the funeral home when Ash went to pick up my urn."

"They are around. Avoid them."

I wanted to keep asking questions, but I was worried I'd drive him away. I was living in this world; I didn't feel like I understood at all. But I was trying to remember he had been dead for a long time.

"They should have a book with all the information about ghosts." I joked.

"There are no ghost writers, unfortunately, Sita. I've always believed that the biggest punishment is that none of us can make art. A few can sing, but the painters, the writers, and the musicians are all forever lost."

"Did you do any of that?"

"I played guitar. It was the only thing that ever brought me true joy."

I wasn't sure what brought me joy anymore. I looked at Ash.

"At least you can still hear music," I said, grasping at the false hope required in darker conversations.

He shrugged, "I feel grateful I ever could play. Sometimes you have to live off of a memory."

"Sometimes, you can't escape it." James looked to Ash too.

"Things will get better. But even if they don't. You've got what?" He looked Ash up and down. "60 years tops. That's like a blink of time when you are dead. You will have so much to do and be when you are free to roam."

"Is any of it even worth it?"

"There aren't choices here, Sita. You can't decide whether to be dead or alive. You can't decide not to have been murdered and to experience a different afterlife. This is our afterlife; you can only choose to enjoy it or hate it. That decision will also determine the ghost you will become."

"What do you mean?"

"You made choices when you were alive. Were you a good person?"

"I like to think so." I played with a tear in my shirt. The question had haunted me for many years.

"Well, you have a new life now, dead girl. You can decide if you will be a good ghost or a bad one. But it's much more difficult than it was when you were living. Your hate, your way of thinking, and your pain, it will win. Ghosts who feed these emotions fall into the darkness. The dark is easy, it wants you, and it will call out to you. You will deteriorate into someone you never were, something you aren't. You won't see it; you'll just be different one day."

"And if I don't want that?"

"Then you..." He put his hand on mine, and it went right through but somehow made me feel comforted. "You have a fight ahead of you, dear girl. You have to fight the bad if you want to be good."

"I think it will be easier when I'm not with Ash any longer."

"You think being with your killer will be easier?" he asked, pulling his hand back.

I shrugged. "Honestly, maybe."

"You might be right. If you fight to stay good, then one day, the fight won't be so hard. I think you would enjoy one of the nature communities."

I pictured ghosts living together out in the woods. Laughing and telling stories about their lives, realizing that they probably had more stories about their dead lives than they did about when they were alive. It made me consider that one day my time living would seem like a day in my life. One day I may forget it altogether.

"It sounds nice."

"The easiest way to stay good is to be out in nature. It always brings out the purest in people."

"Something to look forward to," I responded, smiling at James. " I appreciate all your help, James. It's nice to just not be alone sometimes. No one is constant here beside Ash." I looked at James desperately. "Could you stay? Help me navigate the world? Help me solve a murder."

"Have you ever helped a friend move into a new home?"

"No," I said, knowing I would never help someone with anything like that. I would never move into a new home myself.

"What about loaned a friend some money?"

"No, I guess not," I said.

"Well, that's kind of what the afterlife is like. Everyone is moving, and everyone needs something. I had to draw my line many years ago. You can't help every ghost you come across. I think if I did, I wouldn't be really helping anymore. I'd lose too much of myself, and my advice wouldn't be as pure. I have to let you do this all on your own. I'm sorry, darling."

I felt embarrassed. I knew it was a crazy request to begin with. Who would want to be trapped when they were already free? I pictured myself solving the murder, living with, and haunting the killer, and fighting the evil in me for years and years. When it was over, I'd want to just live. I'd probably have to say no to some poor ghost in the baby years of her ghost life. It would be easier said than done. One day when I would move on, I would first see if I could save Kyra. But I knew it would be too late.

"I understand, James. I hope you'll still come to visit. I

don't know how long I'll be here. It could be a week, or it could be until he retires." I laughed.

"Well, I'll always come by and check anyway. I enjoy these visits. I hope things get better for you, I really do. I can tell you it will be just fine. A pretty and strong girl with many questions will always be ok."

"That's sweet, James." I felt a little heat in my cheeks that made me uncomfortable. So, I noticeably shifted my body, facing Ash again, and awkwardly looked over to him to remind James that I was taken. I was open to an unspoken feeling of something between us. But his compliment made it feel spoken, and I felt ashamed that I might have liked it a little.

"I better get going." He said, standing up.

"James..." I said, standing. "I really hope that you come back, and we can watch another movie together. Maybe one day, when I am free, we will go on another adventure too." I said, fumbling to say the right thing.

I spent the next three nights thinking about those last words. I worried about whether he thought I was crazy. Whether he thought I wasn't interested in him. I wasn't interested. Could I even be interested in James? There was a possibility that I read the whole situation wrong, which was even worse. I acted like James had hit on me when he had just said one nice thing.

Admittedly, it did have me thinking about love in the afterlife. Did love exist between the dead, or was that just another thing I would never have again? Maybe like art, love is something you can only have when you're living.

18

Move

Wednesday, Ash's phone kept ringing. His face grew white as he took a deep breath and answered it. I didn't hear what Detective Ronaldson said. I could have gone in closer and listened, but there was a part of me, a strong part, hoping I wouldn't leave Ash. Now that it was right in front of me, I didn't have the bravery to find out more. So, I just sat and listened to Ash's side of the conversation.

"Do you have evidence?"

"Yes, she loved that bridge."

"Well, that sounds like he did it...How about in ten minutes?"

He hung up and burst into tears. I cuddled into him closer and wondered how long I would be here. I pictured I could just poof away at any minute. I could be next to my killer in a moment, so I held on to him as hard as I possibly could. I knew that these tears were different. These were tears of relief. He had a chance at a real answer. He sucked back in his tears and choked down his pain, wiping the tears away aggressively with my plaid cardigan.

When we arrived at the police station, Ash took a moment to himself in his car. I put my hand over his and reached to try to turn the radio on, but this time, it happened. It was the first time I purposefully communicated with him. It was never like this, something I had control over. I was almost too excited to notice him hitting the radio with his fist until it was bleeding.

"Ash, it's ok. I'm sorry." I said, hoping this wouldn't be our last interaction.

He reached into the back of the car, grabbed a hoodie, put it on, and pulled the sleeves over his cut hands. I stepped out of the car and gave him some space. When he came out, he seemed calm, and I got closer to him again. I could admire him and love him in our last moments together, but I had to stop trying to communicate with him.

We entered the station, and Detective Ronaldson was sitting hunched over his phone, scrolling through something in the lobby. He looked up when Ash entered.

"Good. I was hoping you would get here." He said as he got up and touched Ash on the shoulder. Ash flinched a bit and responded.

"I need a band-aid." He said, moving the sleeve and showing the small cuts.

"Well, looks like you do, son." He motioned towards a police officer and asked him to wrap Ash up and meet him in his office.

After the police officer wrapped up Ash's cuts, he took him to a large brown door with a golden name.

Det Donald Ronaldson

The officer opened the door for Ash, and he entered.

The office had a large window that reached out from a beautiful tree all the way to some mountains in the background. Right in front of the window was a large shiny black leather chair where Detective Ronaldson was sitting. He adjusted his mustache and gave Ash a smile. "Take a seat, son." He said, pointing at one of the fancy velvet gray chairs in front of his desk. Ash sat, and Ronaldson continued. "We, of course, had to contact Sita's aunt first. Although Sita was eighteen, we are still seeing her as the first level of contact. That's why we waited to call you. Hope you understand." He leaned over and pulled a file out from the drawer.

"What happened?" Ash asked, picking at the bandages on his hand.

"Well, we have mentioned Elias Murphey to you before. He is currently going down for three counts of murder. When this happens, we tend to push to make a deal and see if he can tell us about other murders he might have committed."

"And he admitted to Sita's?'

"He did."

"So, this is all done?"

Detective Ronaldson shifted a bit in his chair. "I don't want to get your hopes up too much, Ash. There have been instances when serial killers want a name for themselves, and they admit to murders that they weren't involved in."

"Well, do you think that's what is happening here?"

"I think this is promising. He was in the city at the time

and doesn't have an alibi. He would use the drugs to lure in the victims. I can tell you we think this is enough to charge him."

Ash responded, "Why'd he pick Sita?"

"That's hard to say, son. We will still be doing work on this case until the court date. We need you to write about how her death has impacted you. I don't imagine you will have a hard time doing that." He said, motioning to Ash's bandaged hands with a small laugh.

Ash dropped his head into his hands and gathered himself a moment.

"Ok, I can do that. Do you have any other information?"

"Not right now. But you will be the first to know." He laughed, "Well, the second."

I rolled my eyes for both of us as Ash got up.

"Thanks." He said as he headed towards the door.

Ash left the station and returned home. When he got home, he didn't go to his room. He knocked on his mother's door, and when no one answered, he slowly opened it. Ash entered the room and found that his mother must have stopped by. The room smelt like cigarettes, clothes covered the dirt-brown carpet, and leftover fast food trashed across the bed. He began by throwing clothes one piece at a time into the corner of the room.

Once he could walk through the room, he walked to her closet and opened it. He went straight to the coat and slowly pulled out my car keys. He took a moment to hold them tight in his hand and then left. Then we were back in his car, and we were driving.

"Ash, will we ever know why your mom had those, and where are we going?"

Then I realized he might be ready to finally turn them into the police. It wasn't all that suspicious that my keys were at the house I basically lived in. Plus, now that they had confirmed I was murdered by this stranger, they wouldn't come for his mother.

I was surprised when we didn't arrive at the police station, but instead at a parking spot to view the river. He got out of the car with my keys in his pocket, and I followed. The area was about 20 feet above the roaring river, and he looked down at it. I looked down for a moment, too; the violent water thrashing through the sharp rocks gave me a memory I couldn't quite reach.

He took the keys out of his pocket and ran his finger over the puff, and stared at them as if maybe I was in them. Here he was admiring keys, and I could be attached to Elias at any minute. Then he pulled back and threw the keys as far into the river as he could. I watched them vanish as the waves swallowed them. As soon as he threw them, he turned around and returned to the car. But I stayed. I looked at the river, and where he threw the keys and only left, once I was forced back into the car.

I was angry at Ash on the way back home. But I didn't say a word and tried not to move so I wouldn't scare him because I knew I already put him through so much. I could understand him not wanting them to come for his mother. It could even make convicting the right killer harder if the wrong people found out about it. So, instead, I waited, waited to be pulled to Elias and away from the only person I ever loved.

We arrived back at the house, and Tony's white truck was where Ash normally parked in the driveway. Ash pulled the Jeep into the street and got out. I felt terrible knowing the last thing he needed at this moment was to deal with Theresa or Tony. He entered the house and found Tony sitting on the couch, watching TV with dark eyes focused like he was really trying to solve something even though he watched a comedy show. Ash's voice made him jump.

"Where's my mom?"

He looked over at Ash without moving his body at all.

"Where were you, boy?"

"I don't see how that's any of your business Tony. You aren't my father, and even if you were, I'm 19 now."

Tony laughed and leaned back in the chair.

"I'm just messing, man. She is upstairs in her room. Speaking of, why were you in her rohoon today?" He leaned forward more seriously.

"What's it to you, Tony?"

Tony stood up and walked closer to him. "You know, boy, maybe it was a good thing that bitch died. You ever think about that? Because maybe it's time for you to move on, you know, and leave." Ash's hands clenched into fists. But the sound of his mother's door closing hard made both the men flinch. His mother started down the stairs, and Tony turned back around and flopped onto the couch awkwardly.

Theresa was slower than usual. She wasn't her normal drunk self and looked like she was probably also high on something.

"Ash, welcome ovrr."

Ash responded and held out his arm to help his mother down the stairs. " I live here, mom."

"Not anymore," Tony mumbled from the couch.

He looked back to his mom, and she slowly raised her left hand limply to show a pink plastic ring on her finger. "We are getting married, Ash."

"And we think you should move out," Tony added.

"Happily," He said as he pushed past his mom and walked upstairs. I imagined he hadn't checked on his mother more because he needed to learn to focus on himself at some point. He cared so much for her, but there was only so much he could do.

A few minutes later, he heard Tony and Theresa leave the house. He went into the cabinet and pulled out a shoebox. I decorated it with magazine pictures of different places I wanted Ash and I to visit. Every week we both put money into the box. He sat down and counted out about 800 dollars. He threw it back in the box, placed the box on to the dresser, and stared at it. I sat down and stared at the box too, wondering why I was still here, wondering if he would be ok without me.

19

❧

Solved

Ash rolled over and looked at the ceiling, gripping his hair so tight it seemed he would pull it all out. He opened his phone again and called Emma. I pulled back from him when I saw that. This was it. My final moments with him and I would be spending it listening to him talk to his new girlfriend.

"They found him." He said, wiping away his tears.

"The serial killer, Elias, admitted to the crime."

"I'm ok," he paused. "I'm just happy. It's all over."

"I don't need you to."

"Ok, I'll meet you at the diner on 34th. I guess I need some food."

He hung up and grabbed his own keys off the counter. On his way out the front door, he paused at his mother's room and then grabbed the door handle, shut the door, and kept moving to his car. I felt blessed to be with him. Every moment I knew was stolen. I stared at him and tried to immortalize his perfect face into my memory. I slowly felt more distant from Ash recently, but now that I knew our time was limited, all my bad thoughts were buried.

"*I love you, baby. I'm sorry if I ever hurt you. I won't be here for much longer. I will always be with you in spirit. It's just a break.*"

I touched his face. "*I think we both need a little break from this torment. I'll find a way to leave, though. I will have an eternity to figure out how to find you again. No matter what situation I am in, I will always love you.*"

By the time we arrived at the restaurant, I started to grow concerned that I hadn't left yet. I kept looking at my hands to see if they were fading. I would look at Ash every couple of moments to see if he was still there.

We walked into the small diner that was dripped in white décor. Emma sat at a small table for two with a candle in the middle. Her hair was flowing down in a high ponytail, looking as stupidly beautiful as ever. She had a steaming coffee in front of her as she read the menu. When Ash walked up and took a seat, she immediately set the menu down and gave him all her attention.

"I'm so happy to see you," Emma said in her sing-song voice.

"You too, babe."

Ew.

"Are you ok?"

I hated her, but also, I couldn't wait to talk to someone again. I sat on his lap directly in front of his face.

"I'm ok, Emma. I'm excited we solved it. I think I should be leaving any moment now." I responded without any normal amount of hesitation.

She took a breath.

"Sorry, Ash," emphasizing the Ash. "Something was in my ear." She said, faking to rub her ear a bit. "I didn't hear your response. Are you ok?"

"I'm ok." He answered. "I'm happy it's done. This man deserves the rest of his life in prison."

"You think he for sure did it?"

I waited for his response.

"Everything matches up, Emma, this guy did this. Everything points to him. Then he admitted it. It's over." He paused, "No one else did it."

Then I stood up and looked at him.

"Why say that, Ash?"

I began wondering again why I hadn't left yet. Then I started remembering the keys. I grew angry quickly, and their table trembled.

Emma quickly held it still and smiled, "Oops, I must have picked an uneven table."

"Why would you say no one else did it?! Why am I still here?! Do you still think your mother could have done this?!"

"Ok, calm down," Emma said.

"I think I'm pretty calm," Ash responded.

"Oh, no, sorry." She leaned forward and placed her hand on his. "I know you're calm. I meant... uh ... maybe he could calm down in prison."

I enjoyed watching the mismatched words fall from her mouth. Watching her perfection deteriorate for a slight second. Just then, the waiter walked up—a man covered in tattoos, with a small goatee. I paced the patio as he spoke to them. I quickly returned after he had left and begun speaking straight in Emma's face.

"He found something."

She swatted at me like I was a fly.

"So, what's next?" She asked Ash.

I waited for the answer.

"They pushed up the trial. It's in 2 weeks."

"So soon." She said, twirling her hands through her pony-tail. "And will you go?"

"I don't know. They want me to testify. They want me to explain how much this has impacted my life. I told them I would think about it."

He paused and looked to his left, thinking.

"I'll do it. I'll do it for her. Anything to help them prose-cute him. "

I turned back to Emma and put my face right in front of hers again.

"He found my car keys in his mother's jacket. I think the serial killer did it. But what if he suspects his mother had something to do with it? Why haven't I left if I know who murdered me? Emma, you have to help me. I saw him throw away the evidence into the river. Why would he do that?"

I knew she was listening to me this time because it created a long awkward silence that he burst.

"Anyway, that will be done."

He now moved his own hand toward hers and held it tightly.

"Now, you and I can move on." She replied. Then she added, "Now she can move on."

It was confirmed. Emma was the shiny new member of the giving up on Sita club. She was engulfed in Ash, and I wondered if she knew that he was still mine. She could have him, but he would always be mine. I wanted to tell her this. I wanted to remind her that he would be with me if I wasn't dead. But I didn't say a word.

When we left, I was surprised when Emma came into the car with us. I moved to the back reluctantly. I was not wanting to risk scaring him by sitting too close to him but also not wanting to sit in the same seat as Emma. I tried to will myself away. Tried to tell myself over and over again that this man had done it. Elias killed me.

They returned to Ash's house, and I feared for what would come next. Which trauma they would impose on me once we entered the house. They went up and into his room and laid on the bed. I stood there, awkwardly. I was hoping with all my heart that my stare would make it impossible for Emma to do anything with my boyfriend in front of me.

But she surprised me. She sat up and crossed her legs and faced Ash.

"What about your mom?"

I thought Emma was done with me. But I guess she couldn't be. I was always going to be right here unless she found out the truth. She was risking their whole relationship. I wasn't sure if she was doing it for them or for me, but I didn't care. Ash got up off the bed and stared down at Emma.

"What do you mean, what about my mom, Emma?"

She softened her shoulders and voice. "How is she?"

He softened a bit but kept his almost aggressive stance. "She's fine. She drinks a lot. She isn't a great mom. But that's it. That's all there is to her. Why?"

She hesitated but said with a firmer tone, "Did she get along with Sita?"

Emma was done beating around the bush. She was done hinting and digging.

"No, but I don't see why any of this is your business."

She shifted. "I'm sorry. I didn't know that would upset you. Are you sure everything is ok, Ash?"

He quickly walked to the bed and got very close to her, as she flinched.

"I said, everything was ok. I don't see what my mom has to do with it."

I was proud of Emma suddenly. His anger seemed to motivate her more.

She started questioning him with bold eyes, "You don't think she could have anything to do with her death?"

He grabbed her by the upper arms and pulled her up off the bed. I ran over as if to break up the fight. I looked down at his fingers, pressing deeply into her skin. It felt familiar.

"Why the fuck would you even say something like that?" He said with a tight jaw.

She took a breath. Pulled her manicured hands up and unpeeled his fingers from her skin. He didn't resist and put his hands back down.

"Why so defensive?" She said.

"I told you already! "He yelled this time. "They caught the guy who did it! It's none of your fuckin business anyway!" She stepped back.

"Feels like you're not telling me something, Ash."

"Emma, I think you should go." He said with his hands clenched into fists by his side.

"Ash, I think you should be honest with me."

He quickly brought out his hand and almost grabbed her

neck. She moved just in time and ran out of the room. I heard his mother's door slam shut and lock. I looked at Ash as he grew redder and breathed like he was trying to expel something from his throat. I went into his mother's room to find Emma. She was looking around at her options. The window was blocked by the bed, a way to keep the room dark. It was large and oak, and it would be impossible for her to move without help.

"What are you doing?" I asked as she moved towards the closet. She started rifling through the pockets of all of Theresa's jackets.

"Something weird is going on here, Sita. Something isn't right."

I realized that Emma was looking out for me. Ever since my parents died, I pushed everyone away but Ash. I didn't really believe we needed other people in our lives. But maybe, I needed her, perhaps love wasn't enough, and you needed friends too. I walked around the room, looking for anything to help her, looking for a way that this was all wrong and that this whole thing was a misunderstanding. But also I was thinking about how we could keep Emma out of this. All I wanted was to cause people less pain, and all I was doing was creating more.

Heavy knocks on the door broke up the room.

"Emma," he said with a calm voice. "Come on out of there. Let's talk about this."

"Emma, he isn't himself. I think you should stop searching and get out of here. I'm scared that he would do almost anything to protect his mother." I said.

"No, Sita. I can't just leave right now. I'm your only shot, and if something this terrible happened, the truth has to come out." She pointed at the door. "And Ash is clearly showing that he actually knows something. Before, I thought this would be easy. We could find some logical reason you were killed. But I can't live with the fact that Ash knows more than he's letting on."

I saw a side of her for a moment that I wondered if even existed in me at all. She had power; she was more focused on her mission than her relationship. The power of choosing the right thing over love was a power most would never know. After seeing her do it, I knew it was possible, and it made me feel powerful too. She turned to the door as he banged on it harder now.

"What are you doing in there?!" He shouted. "Open the fucking door, Emma."

She responded this time, and her soft voice had become almost sinister, "I just needed a minute, Ash. I'm not doing anything."

She took a breath and walked towards the door.

Emma left Ash's mother's room. She pushed her way past Ash back into his room and stood in front of the bed. Her posture was tall, straight, and demanding. Ash walked in after her, facing her in the same matter. The color had returned to his face, but his eyebrow stayed curved downward.

I looked back and forth between them. This was a moment I would leave Ash. If Emma successfully revealed the true sinister nature of his mother. I could be gone in a moment.

"What is going on here, Ash? Why are you covering for your mother? Where are the keys?" She asked calmly. His eyes grew wide.

"You bitch." and with full force, he pushed her to the floor. It happened so fast it didn't even feel like a moment, I watched her drop to the ground heavily, and the floor shook a bit.

She looked around quickly as he began to kneel above her. He trapped her by sitting on her. I jumped in between them.

"Ash, what are you doing? All for your mother?! You hate her!" I pulled unsuccessfully at his shoulders as he stared down at her.

But she didn't need my help; she saw something, something dark under the bedside table. He leaned his whole weight on to her.

"I need you to stop right now." He said, looking at her in a new sinister way. He looked at her right hand as she pulled it up to distract him. He grabbed it by the wrist. Her left hand slid under the nightstand and pulled something out. Then she made a face of relief as if she was saved.

She sprayed him in the eyes with black pepper spray. My missing black pepper spray. Ash fell back, clutching at his eyes. Emma stumbled up and started running. I didn't take my eyes off of Ash as Emma ran, and I heard the front door close behind her. I stayed with Ash only because there was no other choice.

Ash stumbled up and ran to the bathroom and jumped in the shower with all his clothes on. I stayed there. I stared at the floor, trying to make sense of everything at first, then trying to make sense of anything. Ash got out of the shower and quickly put new clothes on. Finally, as he pulled out a backpack and started to pack it, I spoke. *"Ash, Ash, why do you have my pepper spray?"*

He looked at the time on his phone and threw more clothes inside. He rubbed his burning red eyes, and I thought for a moment that I saw a tear. I couldn't decide if it was for him or for me. He ran to the bathroom and began grabbing things like his toothbrush. I followed him into there.

"Ash, did your mom leave that there too?"

He opened the box of our money he counted earlier. He pulled it out and straightened it. Then he rolled it into a ball and secured it with a hairband of mine he grabbed from the drawer. He threw the money into the bag and zipped it up.

"Ash, wait!" I yelled and pounded at him. He paused. He put his hand towards where I had hit him.

I stopped too.

"Please, Ash, I love you. I'm sure you can explain what is going on."

A tear escaped his eye, which he quickly wiped off. He grabbed his bag, and ran downstairs and got into the car. He was moving so fast, and I couldn't help but move with him. I needed to stop. I needed to process. We got in the car, and he pulled out of the driveway. Then he suddenly stopped and threw it in the park. He ran back inside and got the picture of us out of the nightstand drawer. He grabbed it roughly and threw it in the back of the car. He drove stone-faced in one direction, towards the highway that leads out of town.

I didn't say another word. I watched him. I watched him pull over after about an hour of driving in front of an empty field. I watched him take the phone and throw it as far as he could. Then get back in the car and drive away like nothing happened.

We drove in silence. I surrendered. I didn't want to know

anything anymore. I didn't want to be here. I didn't want to think and solve anymore. For just a while, I needed a break. I presumably had an eternity here, so for once, I didn't want to rush.

After hours that felt like years, I saw a blue sign with a sun in the middle, "Welcome to Arizona." I looked at Ash, who I felt had kidnapped me. He rubbed his tired eyes and began searching for somewhere to stop. Another 30 minutes and we saw a motel's glowing sign with vacancy. He pulled over, and we left the car. It was dark, and the shine from the motel light felt blinding in the night. I saw two ghosts walking around the outside of it. One was a little boy, and the other was a man with a long grey beard. They stopped and looked at me. I felt cold, and I thought I could hear a distant growl.

I was relieved as Ash pulled me into the lobby, and the ghosts couldn't look at me any longer. The lobby was as run down as the building. The musty green walls felt like they perfectly matched my new distorted dead life. He went to the front desk and slammed some cash on the counter. The women working looked like she had lived through a lifetime of meth. The cash he placed was almost double the amount of a room.

"One room, one night, no questions."

She looked at him deeply, then turned and handed him a key for room 12. When we entered, it smelled musty like a wet towel, and I had a strong feeling we shouldn't be there. He sat down in an old chair by the window and pulled maps out from his backpack.

I stared at him. *"Ash, what is going on? "*

I was desperate for answers but felt destined for none.

I looked around the room, at a phone on the table. Wishing I could call Emma, I walked over and tried to lift it. As I did, the phone fell to the ground. He jumped, the determined look in his eyes quickly shifting back to terror.

"It's me!" I said this time with power borrowed from Emma. *"Why are you always so fucking scared? It's not like I'm haunting you?!"*

But then it hit me. It was like a wrecking ball had come crashing into the desert. Pieces were everywhere, and order was nowhere.

"Because I am." He walked over to the phone and put it back up. *"I'm haunting you."*

He walked back over to the chair, looking back at the phone.

"You killed me."

As the words reluctantly creeped out of my mouth. I saw it. I saw his fingers digging deeply into Emma's skin. I saw those same fingers digging into mine on the bridge- a picture, just for a moment, of his same furrowed brow, the anger in his eyes, the fingers in my skin, the bridge beneath my feet.

The life leaving me and my death approaching. I was destined to forever haunt my murderer if I wasn't guarding a loved one. That's why I was never good at protecting him because I had been haunting him all along. Everything in me changed. The overwhelming love I felt for him was replaced with overwhelming hate within a single moment.

He laid on the bed and closed his eyes after planning our next leg of the trip. I would normally lie with him, try to soothe him. But I knew now that that wasn't my job anymore. It never was. I stood above him on the bed. I felt the anger flood my veins. I crawled over and sat on him; the same way I had watched him sit on Emma.

I pushed all my ghostly weight and held down his arms into the bed. He opened his eyes and moved slightly, feeling the pressure. Then I don't know how, but I shook the entire bed. The creaky old bed rattled and echoed through the room.

Ash jumped up, and his face grew pale as he stared at the bed. He shook himself off and stripped down to jump in the shower. I laid on the bed. Satisfied. Satisfied, I kicked him off. Satisfied, Emma had gotten away. Satisfied that even though the future looked so bleak, at least I knew what it looked like now.

20

ONE DEAD GIRL

Ash has been on the run for five years now. I was never too interested in tracking time. Living girls do it because time is limited, but a dead girl has all the time in the world.

Ash and I watched the news before we made it out of the state. There was maybe a thirty-second clip about the search for Ash. They named him as the suspect for an assault but never mentioned me. Detective Ronaldson gave the information, and it seemed he wanted to say more but couldn't. I knew there wasn't much they could do without better evidence. Even if they could prove Ash did it, it was useless unless they could catch him.

I wouldn't want to live out the rest of his life with him in prison. But I would prefer that than to know that other women might die too. I lived by watching Ash closely, especially when he was with other women. I didn't know what my plan was if he were to attack another woman. I regretted not being more helpful for Emma, not being able to fight for her.

This was just another thing in an endless list of things I didn't have control over.

I was lucky to find out about my murder at all. Over the years, I put the pieces together about that day and about who Ash really was. The road got hard on him. He couldn't take being on the run and never telling anyone what had happened. So, he told bits and pieces on his travels.

Usually, he confessed at bars and to strangers late at night. He would always be in a new state leaving only pieces of the puzzle with one drunk in one state before the next piece was laid. We went to Arkansas, and he worked odd jobs in construction for a while. We stayed at another worn-out motel while we were there. This one had a local bar down the street that was always packed. One night he went there with an older man he met at one of the jobs. Ash drank four whiskeys before he turned to the man and said, "I once had a girlfriend who died. She was killed."

He added. "Someone pushed her off the bridge. It was all planned. The killer had someone punch in his time card at work, and he went to the bridge. He pretended he needed something from her purse and stole anything that might have helped her get away." He shook his head and took another shot of whiskey. Then he left the bar, never to return before the man could even question his words.

He went to a college bar in Florida. When a girl tried to come hit on him, he told her that his ex had planned to go to a college out of state and how she was writing about it in her journal. He found out and destroyed the journal. If she wasn't going to be with him, then why would she be anywhere? I brought college up to Ash many times. I never thought it was a question. We would obviously have a long-distance relationship if I got accepted out of state. He never said anything about it. It was almost like he found it easier to murder me than to be honest than to tell me how he felt.

He was almost caught once in Georgia. This time he was hitting on a young girl at the bar. The drunker he got, he accidentally called her Sita. When she threw her drink at him, he lost it. He grabbed her by the neck and slammed her onto the pool table. People at the bar pulled him off and called the police. Ash pulled back with his charming tone and said he was sorry before booking it at the front door, never to be seen in Georgia again.

He confided in a hip bartender in Oregon, the story of a girl in his hometown, who was murdered by her boyfriend. How the boyfriend found out, she was considering leaving him for school. So, he went and bought heroin to make himself look innocent when he killed her. He tucked the heroin tightly into her shoe and said to trust him like it was a gift before he pushed her into the roaring river.

He told a sleeping drunk at a bar in California that if he ever killed anyone, he would hide evidence on someone he didn't like in case he ever needed to frame them. Someone that was making his life more difficult. "Two birds with one stone." He said with a sinister laugh.

He was drunk at a local diner in Washington when a woman accidentally spilled some of her drink on him as she walked to her seat. He grabbed her arm and pulled her in near. "I almost did it. I forgot one thing. I forgot to get rid of one thing. No one would have known I killed her." He stumbled up and left the diner before she had made it back to her table to tell her friends. Two of them ran out the door to follow him. But he was already in the cab on the way to the motel.

All these pieces came together like a train that never felt quite complete but still ran just fine. It released me. Not completely, though, as I would always be stuck to Ash, as long as he lived. But it released me in so many other ways. It allowed me to haunt him without guilt. I enjoyed it now. It liked turning the tv on late at night, ruffling the curtains when he looked peaceful or happy.

But it wasn't just about that. Life wasn't just about Ash anymore. I spent so much of my life and my afterlife obsessed with love, having it, losing it, and needing it. It would have been easy for me to replace that love with hate. But I would keep fighting to be good. I would keep fighting over the emotions that threatened to take me over.

I knew he would likely die soon. I watched him live more and more unhealthy, and he still mourned his freedom. But some people were lucky, and maybe I would be haunting Ash for many years. If there was one thing I knew for sure, it was that I was rarely in control of my situation.

But I wasn't going to wait for a new one anymore. When my parents died, I let myself soak in sadness and isolation. Whenever I got into a bad situation, I let it pull me down with a violent grip. I was alive for eighteen years. I have been dead for about six. So, I made a choice, a choice to start living my dead life better. I became obsessed with showing myself that one dead girl is just as valuable as one alive girl, and both are enough all on their own.

CPSIA information can be obtained
at www.ICGtesting.com
Printed in the USA
LVHW050907161120
671800LV00003B/370

9 780578 783468